STROKE OF MIDNIGHT

*Three stories in one
by three sizzling Blaze authors!*

Jamie Denton

"With a unique flair for combining a sexy,
sultry love story with an intense plot, Denton
once again proves her mastery of romance."
—*WordWeaving.com*

Carrie Alexander

"A gifted writer with a fresh, distinctive voice,
Carrie Alexander crafts an exquisite love story
pulsing with a blazing intensity and sensuality
every reader will savor."
—*Romantic Times*

Nancy Warren

"Put the gloves on for Nancy Warren's latest
because it will definitely sizzle your fingertips with
highly sensual scenes, wicked, larger-than-life
characters and an intriguing premise."
—*Romantic Times*

Blaze™

Dear Reader,

What happens when three Harlequin Blaze authors create three rocking Blaze heroines who meet three luscious Blaze men of their wildest dreams? Triple the story, triple the fun and...triple the pleasure!

Jamie Denton starts off with a sizzling romance of sexy revenge. Tired of having her heart broken, *Impulsive* fashion reporter Natalie Trent takes advantage of a golden opportunity to exact a little revenge on her last prince-turned-frog. But how can she keep her heart safe when the frog in question is quite possibly the man of her dreams?

Carrie Alexander's tale begins when Isabel Parisi hooks up with a masked man for a very *Enticing* champagne celebration. But is Isabel's midnight lover the complete stranger she believes, or is he a friend hoping to win her heart?

Nancy Warren's heroine, accountant Arianne Sorenson, always counts the cost of everything. Can she take the ultimate risk and fall in love with the *Tantalizing* man who's the stuff of fantasies—even if the cost is everything?

We had a fabulous time working together on our linked stories, and hope that you enjoy your New Year celebration as much as our characters did, long after the *Stroke of Midnight*.

Happy New Year!

Jamie, Carrie and Nancy

P.S. To enter the *Stroke of Midnight* contest, visit our Web sites at www.jamiedenton.net, www.carriealexander.com, and www.nancywarren.net.

STROKE OF MIDNIGHT

Jamie Denton
Carrie Alexander
Nancy Warren

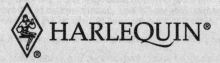

HARLEQUIN®

TORONTO • NEW YORK • LONDON
AMSTERDAM • PARIS • SYDNEY • HAMBURG
STOCKHOLM • ATHENS • TOKYO • MILAN • MADRID
PRAGUE • WARSAW • BUDAPEST • AUCKLAND

For Jennifer Green, our favorite heroine.

ISBN 0-373-79118-6

STROKE OF MIDNIGHT

Copyright © 2003 by Harlequin Books S.A.

The publisher acknowledges the copyright holders
of the individual works as follows:

IMPULSIVE
Copyright © 2003 by Jamie Ann Denton.

ENTICING
Copyright © 2003 by Carrie Antilla.

TANTALIZING
Copyright © 2003 by Nancy Warren.

CONTENTS

PROLOGUE

Prologue

New Year's Eve, 2002
Home of Raphael Monticello, New York City

"HAPPY FREAKIN' NEW YEAR," said Arianne Sorenson, raising a flute of champagne to no one in particular.

It was an hour past midnight and the annual New Year's Eve party at the home of famous shoe designer Rafe Monticello continued in full swing, but back here at the marble-and-gilt bar, there was only her, eleven empty bar stools and an Italian bartender who didn't speak much English.

"Back at you, girlfriend!"

Arianne was so surprised to hear another female answer her that she turned rather suddenly on her bar stool and nearly toppled off onto her Dolce-&-Gabbana-clad butt.

"Natalie Trent," the redhead said. "Mind if I join you?" Not waiting for an answer, she hoisted herself onto an adjacent stool and carefully set a signature gold shoe box on the bar.

Arianne supplied her name, deciding she liked her new friend's direct approach.

Natalie tugged the hem of her black sequined skirt down a notch. "What are we drinking to?" She signaled the bartender for another champagne.

Arianne considered the question seriously. Before she

could come up with a toast that simultaneously expressed present misery but left the door open for future bliss, another female voice broke into her thoughts, this one pitched lower than the first.

"Are we all playing wallflower? Great. I need a breather." The third woman joined them, carelessly adjusting the plunging neckline of the unbuttoned man's dress shirt she wore tucked into a fringed miniskirt. Mascara was smudged beneath her exotic eyes and lipstick blurred the shape of her mouth.

It was clear she'd been involved in more than the ceremonial New Year's Eve kiss.

Arianne leaned closer and whispered, "You have a tuxedo shirt stud in your hair."

With a husky laugh, the woman flipped her dark hair over her face, shaking out the stud. It fell onto the bar and she gazed at it with a small smile playing over bee-stung lips. "I always like to keep a party memento."

"From a stud of a different kind, no doubt." Arianne suppressed a sigh.

Everyone else always seemed to get lucky on New Year's Eve.

"Pour another one, honey," the brunette said to the bartender, who obligingly filled a third flute with Rafe Monticello's vintage French champagne. As the bubbly liquid foamed, Natalie introduced herself and Arianne.

"Isabel Parisi," the third woman replied, popping the stud into her evening bag before accepting her own glass.

"Arianne was just making a toast," Natalie said.

The two women looked to Arianne expectantly, as though this were her bar and these her guests. Not wanting to appear like a lonely loser when they were both obviously having a much better time than she, Arianne skipped the present misery part and went straight for future bliss. "Here's to fulfilling our dreams," she said.

"Fulfilling our dreams," the others echoed as they clinked glasses.

Natalie and Arianne took ladylike sips.

Isabel drained her champagne in one long gulp. "We should smash our glasses against the fireplace to make our wishes come true."

"Oh, no. You can't!" Arianne cried. "These are stem crystal. Seventy-eight dollars a glass at Saks."

Because the other two were blinking at her as though she were under the illusion she was a contestant on *The Price Is Right*, she rapidly explained.

"I'm Rafe Monticello's accountant. I see all the bills."

"It must cost him a pretty penny to give away hundreds of pairs of Monticellos every year as party tokens," said Natalie.

Arianne shuddered. "You don't want to know."

In the past few years, Rafe had put his Harvard MBA to work launching his Italian mother's shoe designs in America. Since he became CEO, the company had gone from outrageous success to outrageous success. Blahnik, Choo and Monticello were the trio to make any shoe fetishist drool.

Natalie pointed to the pair of Monticellos on Arianne's feet—the ones from last year's party. "I saw those on Fifth Avenue for six hundred retail."

Arianne nodded. "Even the wholesale price is more than I would ever spend on shoes."

"I'd just as soon go barefoot." Isabel crossed her long bare legs, lounging against the bar. She wore simple beaded ballerina flats. "But if we must put on killer stilettos, why not do it in style, courtesy of Rafe? He can afford the indulgence."

"Beats going home alone." Natalie let out a weighty sigh. "Again."

They sipped for a while in silence.

"Well, aren't we the cliché," Isabel observed. "A blonde, a brunette and a redhead. Three single chicks, sitting at a bar."

"You're single?" Natalie blinked and then looked briefly at the bag containing the stud's stud.

Noticing the direction of her glance, Isabel said, "Are we talking tonight or for life?"

"Aren't they the same?"

"Uh-uh. I love being single. I came here for the fine selection of French champagne and Italian men. *Bellissimo.*" Isabel kissed her fingertips at the bartender, who winked at her.

"Si, Bella," he replied.

She turned toward the other women. "How about you two?"

"Fashion reporter," Natalie explained. "I pretty much had to kill to get an invitation, but it was worth it. I get to hang out with people I want to interview, and take home a pair of Monticellos." She smoothed her hand adoringly over the gold box.

Arianne shrugged. "It's my job. Rafe is an important client. I come to make nice." She lifted a foot in the air and let the light catch the soft gleam of expensive leather. "And I come for the Monticellos."

"Don't tell me you both prefer the shoes to the men," Isabel teased.

"Hmm," Natalie murmured, then drained the last of her champagne. "At least shoes only hurt your feet."

Recognizing one another as veterans of the Manhattan dating wars, the three women shared looks of commiseration.

Isabel brightened her wry smile before their private party cycled downward into pity. "I'm in fashion, too." She preferred to stick to career talk rather than explain her colorful history with men. "Fabric designer. I've been working with the Monticellos on their spring line."

This spurred a lively discussion of who they knew in common, the upcoming Fashion Week and what was happening among the rich and famous fashionistas.

By the time they were ready to leave, they'd become friends. Isabel was already inviting them to a post-party rehash at her Elizabeth Street loft near SoHo for New Year's day brunch. Natalie was working out how to use Arianne's influence to get an exclusive interview with Lucia Monticello, the shoe designer and Rafe's mother, and Arianne was trying to come up with a polite way to ask Isabel how she managed to show up at a party, get laid and still go home single.

They decided to share a taxi. As they prepared to leave the bar, Natalie pulled the others into a three-way hug and declared, "We have to make a solemn vow that if we're all still single next year, we'll do this again."

"No man's catching hold of me," Isabel said with a saucy wink. "I'm in."

"My engagement just ended a year ago," Arianne said. "I'm sure I'll be here."

Natalie paused. "Look. I met someone tonight—" she bit her lip "—but he kind of disappeared. If he doesn't reappear and sweep me off my feet in the next three hundred and sixty-four days, I'm in, too."

"Swear it on your Monticellos!"

Solemnly, each of them placed a hand on the distinctive gold shoe box and promised.

IMPULSIVE

Jamie Denton

1

One year later

NATALIE TRENT NEEDED to get laid. In the absolute worst possible way, too, she thought, trying not to frown as she swiped mascara over her pale, reddish-blond eyelashes. Not that she hadn't had offers in the past twelve months. She lived in Manhattan, for pity's sake, where the men weren't only plentiful, but plenty horny. She'd just gotten…choosy, all because of a stupid New Year's resolution she'd been determined to keep.

She smoothed the foam applicator of her new "long-lasting" lipstick over her lips, then fanned them with her hand to speed up the drying process. Resolving not to fall in love with every guy she dated might have been a wise decision at the time, but it'd also been the most crippling. Apparently she wasn't wired to spread her legs if she wasn't in love. A small detail she'd come to understand about herself which had made for some very long and lonely nights—three hundred and sixty-five of them to be exact.

Lips dry, she applied the glossy overcoat before slipping both tubes inside her vintage gold Fendi, right next to her engraved invitation to the Monticello Ball. She scooted out of the postage-stamp-size bathroom into the equally small bedroom she used as a dressing room and closet. What her minuscule one-bedroom apartment lacked in space, it more than made up for in location. At least she had the front apartment overlooking 77th Street in the five-story converted town house. She could've found an apartment much less costly with more room, but she wouldn't trade the Upper East Side locale just off Park Avenue any more than she'd part with her beloved Manolo Blahnik, Jimmy Choo or Monticello shoes.

Standing in front of the full-length mirror she'd tacked to the wall next to her shoe armoire, she almost considered changing. The short metallic-gold Anna Molinari shift tested the legal limit of decency. She should wear the black Versace she'd received as a thank-you gift from the designer following a glowing article Natalie had written for *W* on Donatella's spring line, but then the strappy gold, four-inch Monticellos she treasured would have to go, as well.

She turned and frowned at the reflection of her backside. The dress was definitely eye-catching, though, even if it left next to nothing to the imagination.

Wait a minute, she thought. Wasn't that the entire point of wearing the sexy, slinky designer dress? To catch a man's eye and finally put an end to her self-imposed, albeit unintentional, celibacy?

She made one last adjustment to the clingy dress before slipping a thin pair of shoulder-length gold earrings through her lobes. A satisfied smirk tipped her mouth. After five years in New York she'd learned to hide her small-town background. She'd even managed to ditch most of her Pollyanna views and could be as cynical as Isabel—if she tried. But what mattered most was not a single invited guest at the party, other than her two closest friends, would ever guess that the only daughter of the town drunk had dared to cross the lines of privilege and invaded the exclusive territory of the rich and famous.

Armed with her personal invitation to the hottest party in town and a few discreet foil packets, she left her apartment and prayed she'd find not only a cab, but an end to her abstinence. She'd lasted an entire year and hadn't once given her heart away. Little had she known when she'd impulsively made that stupid resolution that a sexless year would result. She'd suffered more than any young, healthy twenty-seven-year-old female ever should. She had needs and she planned to have the desperate edge taken off her razor-sharp libido—tonight. And she would do it without losing her heart in the bargain.

She'd only had to walk as far as Fifth Avenue in the cold night air before she found an available taxi and gave the driver Isabel's address. As a freelance fashion reporter, Natalie treated tonight's event as more of a working party than a social event. The annual Monticello Ball promised plenty of grist for her ''who's who wearing what'' article, from the exquisitely dressed to the *oh, puleeze, what was she thinking?* disasters. Mr. Blackwell she wasn't, but both *Vogue* and *W* would pay her a small fortune for a report on the fashion exploits of the celebrities in attendance at the most anticipated party of the year. She might even wrangle Rafe Monticello into granting her an exclusive preview of the upcoming fall line of Monticello shoes. Or perhaps an interview with the creative whiz behind the empire, his mother, the elusive Lucia.

By the time the cab neared Isabel's loft, Natalie decided if she planned to answer when sexual opportunity banged on her door, she needed to adopt a more free-spirited attitude toward sex like her fabric designer pal,

Isabel Parisi. Isabel had sex all the time and never let her heart get all tangled up in the sheets. Unfortunately, Natalie had a feeling she really had more in common with sensible accountant Arianne Sorenson. Arianne didn't give her heart away, probably because it had already been stolen, Natalie thought. Either her friend wasn't fessing up or she had yet to realize her heart already belonged to the sexy, dark, Rafe Monticello.

Once the cabbie turned down Isabel's street, Natalie pulled out her cell and dialed. Iz picked up on the second ring. "I'm on my way, Natalie."

"On your way downstairs, I hope," Natalie told her. "Arianne will flip if we're late, and the traffic's already horrendous."

"What did you expect?" Isabel said. "It's New Year's Eve."

"Just hurry," Natalie said, hating how desperate she sounded. "I don't want to be late, either."

Isabel's chuckle was husky and knowing. "Don't panic, Nat. Your freebie Monticellos will be waiting for you even if we are late."

Natalie disconnected the call. The exclusive Monticellos weren't all she hoped would be waiting for her at the ball. Although she couldn't wait to get her hands on this year's expensive glass slipper, she really hoped to find herself a prince. One ready, willing and more than able to put an end to her year of sexual deprivation.

JOE SEBASTIAN KNEW it was *her* the minute she walked into the ballroom. From his place at the bar, he waited for his lungs to refill with oxygen and his heart to stop ricocheting around in his chest. Time hadn't dulled the images etched on his memory. If anything, they were even sharper now that he'd seen her.

A breathtaking vision wrapped in gold that closely hugged her lethal curves, she was hands-down the most sensual woman in the room as far as he was concerned. Although she wore a gold satin-and-sequined mask, complete with gold plumes sprouting up from the left side, he'd know that body anywhere. He should, since she'd been haunting his fantasies for a full year.

Would she remember him? he wondered, tossing back the last of the scotch and water he'd been nursing the past hour. Without taking his eyes off her, he signaled for the bartender. "Straight up this time," he told the guy. "Better make it a double."

Would she even speak to him? He wouldn't blame her if she smashed one of Rafe's Renaissance urns over his head. No less than he deserved for pulling a disappearing act on her after the time they'd spent alone with a bottle of champagne in one of the upstairs alcoves. No woman liked to feel used, and he imagined that's exactly how Natalie perceived those incredible moments at the stroke of midnight one year ago tonight. Provided she even remembered.

He thanked the bartender and walked back into the ballroom for a closer look at the woman he hadn't been able to erase from his mind. The taste of her mouth, the curve of her hips, the silk of her hair wrapped around his hand were images burned into his memory like a brand. The sound of her throaty laugher as he'd led her to the alcove and closed the dark red velvet drape for privacy. Her purr of pleasure when he'd skimmed his hands over her body and kissed her senseless until they were both filled with a need so fierce it had nearly killed him to walk away from her after offering some lame excuse he couldn't even recall and promising to return shortly.

He'd never heard her outrage because he'd been forbidden to say so much as a goodbye. He'd left, but he'd never forgotten, and for the first time in his career as a naval intelligence officer, he'd been filled with resentment for the oath he'd sworn.

His days of disappearing for months on end were thankfully behind him. After twelve years of serving his country, Joe had had enough of covert operations, security issues and the only semblance of home being the nearest rack on a ship sailing to a classified location.

Acknowledging he was ready to settle in one place and put down roots was one thing. Actually having the staying power to remain in one place for any length of time was another. So had knowing what he'd do for a living. Instead of discharging from the Navy, he supposed he could've accepted the offer to become an instructor for SEAL training and collected a full pension in another ten to fifteen years. While he could always go back to civilian life, he craved solidity. After his last mission, the more distance from a lifestyle he wasn't completely sure he still had faith in, the better. Investigating white-collar crime for the Securities and Exchange Commission did lack a certain level of excitement he'd become accustomed to as a SEAL, but men and women generally weren't tortured or maimed beyond recognition because of corporate greed.

He moved through the couples dancing beneath the frescoed dome until he reached the edge of the dance floor where she only had to glance in his direction to see him. The black leather mask hid his face, but he was arrogant enough to hope she'd still recognize him.

The cool blonde dressed in elegant black standing next to Natalie said something to her that caused Natalie to turn and scan the ballroom. She nodded, spoke to the exotic dark-haired woman beside her, and then looked directly at him. From across the room, he raised his glass slightly and smiled when her clear blue eyes widened beneath her mask. What he could see of her face, paled.

She quickly turned away and spoke to his old friend and host, Rafe. Oh, yeah, he thought. She hadn't forgotten him. From her reaction, she obviously hadn't expected to find him here, either. The night suddenly held a wealth of possibilities.

He tossed back a good portion of scotch that only inflamed the heat already simmering in his belly. At least she hadn't looked as if she wanted to rip his balls off for leaving her the way he had. Maybe she'd allow him to make it up to her by finishing what they started last year.

She left her friends, snatched a glass of champagne from the tray of a passing waiter as if it were a lifeline and started circling the ballroom. He took in the subtle swing of her hips and the enticing movement of her breasts as she slowly headed in his direction. His fingers weren't the only part of his body flexing. Being this close to her, he could see she was even hotter than she'd been in his memories, and they'd been damned hot.

He finished off the last of his drink as Natalie cruised the ballroom as if she owned the place, confident and sexy as hell. He'd been too long at sea if the sight of a woman made his dick this hard. He shouldn't be surprised by his reaction. It'd been the same all year. Despite the little time they'd actually spent together, one thought of Natalie and his libido took off like an F-14 from the deck of an aircraft carrier. The woman had gotten under his skin, something thousands of miles of ocean hadn't cured.

He would've contacted her when he'd returned to the States three months later, but without a last name, he hadn't known how to get in touch with her. Rafe had

been out of the country and before Joe had had an opportunity to speak to him, new orders had been cut and
he'd been shipped out to another classified location. After
nine months of being sent on one mission after another,
then arranging for his discharge and landing a job with
the S.E.C., he'd figured too much time had passed and
he had given up on ever seeing Natalie again. When he'd
accepted Rafe's invitation, he hadn't even considered the
off chance of running into her again. He couldn't believe
his luck that she was actually here, but that didn't nec-
essarily mean he knew the right words to say after so
much time had passed.

Fate wasn't a theory he subscribed to as a rule. Tonight
he'd make an exception—provided she showed him the
slightest hint she was still interested.

She came to a stop a few feet in front of him, sipping
her champagne as she turned and casually scanned the
crowd on the marble dance floor. If it hadn't been for the
surreptitious glances she kept shooting his way, he might
have thought he'd imagined her reaction when their eyes
had met a few moments ago.

The pain it cost him was worth every agonizing ache
as he checked out her ass and those long legs that went
on forever. The hem of her impossibly short gold dress
flirted with her slender thighs. She glanced his way again,
then started tapping her foot as if impatient. The hem of
her dress swayed with the movement, drawing his attention to the shimmering gold dress barely covering her
derrière.

He struggled for breath and stared hard, but couldn't
detect a single panty line beneath the formfitting dress.
Forget breathing. The heavy pounding of his heart convinced him he was close to cardiac arrest.

She spun around suddenly and looked directly in his

eyes. Behind the frilly mask, her eyes held an intriguing combination of curiosity with a dose of apprehension. Unsure what to say to her, he just stared like a tongue-tied recruit and enjoyed the sight of her incredible body, the slight tilt of her head and the sophisticated upswept style of her more strawberry than blond hair.

"Excuse me," she murmured, then took off faster than a missile.

"Damn it," he muttered to himself as she wove her way through the guests and disappeared before he came to his senses.

"You look as if you could use this," Rafe said suddenly from beside him. Amusement filled his voice. "Problems?"

Joe took the glass Rafe offered and downed half the contents. "There won't be if you can tell me the name of that redhead so I don't lose her again."

He and Rafe had been friends since their college days when raising hell and chasing women had been their favorite pastimes. Their hell-raising days had continued long after they'd been handed their Ivy League diplomas, but when it came to the opposite sex, Joe was an amateur compared to Rafe.

"Natalie Trent," Rafe told him.

Joe frowned. "She's not one of your…" A sharp stab of jealousy hit him hard.

"Women?" Rafe finished for him. He chuckled. "No. She's all yours, my friend."

"How do you know her?" He wasn't proud of himself for asking, but he was having a hard time stemming the flow of suspicion despite Rafe's reassurance that he and Natalie had never been involved.

"She's in the fashion industry," Rafe said absently, his attention shifting to the cool blonde Joe had seen earlier with Natalie. He nodded in the other woman's direction. "My accountant, she knows her."

Based on the intensity in Rafe's eyes as he watched the blonde, his friend looked as if he wanted to discuss more than balance sheets with the lovely bean counter.

Once Rafe left him, Joe searched the ballroom for Natalie. Apparently she'd pulled a disappearing act all her own.

He wound his way around the dance floor. A matched set of statuesque brunettes stopped him and smiled with blatant, smoldering interest. The silver-clad bookend on the left held up three fingers while her identical counterpart pointed toward rooms upstairs.

Under normal circumstances, he might have accepted without a second thought. Except tonight there was only one woman capable of holding his interest—an incredibly sexy redhead by the name of Natalie Trent.

2

AN OVERLOAD OF ENDORPHINS spurred by unexpected sexual energy pumped through Natalie, making her heart race and her palms sweat. She'd wanted to find a temporary prince for the night to free her from a year of celibacy, not come face-to-face with the man responsible for her making that crippling resolution in the first place.

She moved blindly through the crowd, her intent to put as much distance between herself and the last man to shatter her fragile heart as possible. Needing time to regain her composure and figure out what to do next, she decided to ignore him. "Good luck," she muttered. How could she ignore a man she hadn't been able to forget? The idea of pretending he didn't exist crossed her mind, but that plan had more holes than a pair of fishnet stockings. Based on her body's reaction after one look in those cashmere-soft gray eyes filled with instant recognition, she had a better chance of surviving the discount boutiques during one of Arianne's bargain-hunting excursions.

She passed a small clique of New York socialites adorned in noteworthy designer originals. Instead of whipping out her miniature tape recorder and taking notes for her article, she was lost in the images of those incredible moments spent in Joe's arms last New Year's Eve. Her fingers itched to sift through all that thick, wavy black hair, to trace the outline of his strong, square jaw, to kiss the tempting tilt of his mouth.

He'd smiled at her, bringing back every single memory of that one incredible night, including how intoxicating he'd tasted. With one long sweeping gaze over that rock-solid body packaged handsomely in Armani, her determination to protect her heart fizzled like champagne bubbles rising to the top of a glass. She might as well carve out her heart and hand it to him now to save him the trouble later.

She let out a gusty sigh of relief when she spied Isabel near the edge of the dance floor, thankfully, albeit unusually, alone. Heading in Isabel's direction, Natalie exchanged her empty glass for a fresh flute from the tray of a passing waiter along the way.

"He's here," she blurted when she reached Isabel.

Her friend blinked at her. "He?" she asked, sounding somewhat impatient.

Natalie guzzled the expensive French champagne as if she and Isabel were throwing down shooters with Arianne during happy hour at their favorite haunt. "Joe." She signaled for the closest waiter and made a grab for two more flutes. Tipping her head back, she swallowed the contents of one before the waiter moved away, then handed him the empty.

"I think he knows it's me, but I ditched him." She knew he knew it was her, which only made her more nervous. The deep breath she sucked down with the same zeal as the champagne did little to still her thundering heart. "Oh, God, I don't know how to handle this, Iz," she said miserably, feeling only slightly woozy from all the bubbly she'd consumed in the last five minutes. "Having my heart trampled again by this guy is not how I want to start the New Year."

"Then don't." Isabel tossed out the words as if it were that simple. For Isabel maybe, but as much as Natalie would've liked, she didn't possess her friend's practical approach to sex—get lucky, have a good time and move on with no morning-after regrets. "He can't hurt you if you don't let him."

The first strains of a waltz rose above the din of conversation. Isabel watched the couples sweeping past. Natalie craned her neck to look for Joe.

Every nerve in her body had come instantly alive and insistently demanding the moment she'd first seen him when she and her friends had arrived at the Monticello mansion. Arianne had pointed out a well-known Hollywood couple arguing, and when Natalie had turned to look, her gaze had landed right on Joe. The past twelve, lonely months had faded away and she'd been transported to the previous New Year's Eve.

Although she had made a habit of believing almost every frog possessed prince potential in the past, she'd never been struck by love at first sight before. But she'd learned all too quickly that her silly dreams of happily-ever-after were nothing more than figments of an overly romantic imagination when he'd disappeared without a trace.

She remembered she had just finished a brief, impromptu interview with a young, up-and-coming menswear designer that night when she'd turned and literally run into the man of her dreams. Her champagne had spilled down the front of his tux and when she'd looked up to apologize, she'd been stunned into silence by the blatant desire smoldering in his gaze. Need had kicked in hard and overruled her common sense. When he'd taken the empty glass from her hand and led her onto the

imported marble dance floor, she hadn't dreamed of pro-
testing.

They'd danced for hours without hardly speaking a
word, although they'd communicated plenty in the way
they'd moved and held each other's gaze. As the countdown to midnight had begun, he held her close and kissed
her deeply.

She shook her head and let out a quiet sigh, remem-
bering how easily she'd been swept away like the ridiculous heroines in the fairy tales she'd clung to for so
long. She and Joe had only met, yet an inexplicable bond
had wholly consumed her. She'd been so certain he'd felt
the same unique connection and that Joe was *the one,*
she'd have wagered her entire shoe collection.

Like a fool, she had gone with him to the alcove upstairs for some privacy and had waited for him to return
when he'd been called away suddenly. Over an hour had
passed before she'd finally faced the truth—Joe had been
the one all right, the one to slip right out the door. His
rejection still stung, she realized as she tapped her fingernail against the half-empty crystal flute.

She wasn't a vengeful person by nature, but she
couldn't help wondering how would he feel if someone
treated him as carelessly as he'd treated her. Better yet,
wouldn't it be fun to turn the tables on him and give him
a taste of his own disappearing act?

She faced Isabel, unable to keep the smile from her
lips. "You know…" she mused, as the reckless, completely impulsive plan took shape in her mind. "How do
you think he'd feel if I didn't remember him?"

Isabel nodded, her gaze filling with renewed appreci-
ation and respect Natalie found way too encouraging for
a woman about to even the score. "Good idea," Isabel

said with a hint of pride. "Wound him where it hurts the most—his ego."

Natalie laughed, feeling legitimately lighthearted for the first time in weeks. Fifty-two of them to be exact. "Men and their egos—such a fragile thing."

"Just be careful," Isabel warned as Natalie turned to put her plan into action. "Don't hand him your own heart in the process."

Natalie straightened, adding a good half inch to her already skyscraper height thanks to her gold heels. "Not a chance," she said with determination. "There's only going to be one heart breaking tonight, and it isn't going to be mine."

She'd had an entire year of practice in keeping her heart safe. One more night ought to be a snap.

JOE DISENTANGLED HIMSELF from the persistent brunette bookends intent on a ménage à trois. There was only one woman who interested him, and he intended to have her in his arms by the stroke of midnight. He checked his watch. A little over an hour until the countdown to the New Year. Time was slipping away fast and he still hadn't found Natalie.

A safe distance away from the determined twins, Joe circled the perimeter of the ballroom until he located Natalie. She spoke briefly to the wives of a senator and the mayor of New York, then moved on to a small group where she chatted animatedly for a good ten minutes before she disappeared into the ladies' room. When she emerged he hung back and watched her flit from group to group of people, but he had the distinct impression she was intentionally ignoring him, courtesy of the furtive glances she kept tossing in his direction.

She stopped to talk with a women's handbag designer,

who just happened to be the sister of a sitcom comedian Rafe had introduced him to earlier. Natalie glanced over her shoulder at him as he started to approach, then quickly handed something to the designer. She beelined it toward Rafe, a high-wattage smile on her face as she approached their host. The sound of her laughter at whatever Rafe had said to her had Joe frowning, until his friend glanced his way and motioned for him to join them.

Rafe gave him a knowing grin. "Natalie Trent," he said by way of a formal introduction when Joe reached them. "Joe Sebastian. I believe you two know each other."

"No, I don't believe I've had the pleasure," she said coolly. She extended her hand as if he were a total stranger despite the recognition in her eyes.

What the hell kind of game was she playing? he wondered. Taking her hand in his, he lifted her fingers to his lips, then turned her hand at the last minute to place a kiss on the silky underside of her wrist. Genuine interest flared in her gaze along with a flash of panic. "The pleasure will no doubt be mutual."

Her sharp intake of breath told him loud and clear she'd understood his meaning. He smiled.

She cleared her throat and gently tugged her hand free. "Thank you again, Rafe," she said turning to look up at his friend.

Rafe nodded. "I'm looking forward to it. Now if you'll excuse me, I'll leave you two to get better acquainted."

"Very charming, isn't he?" Natalie said, watching Rafe walk away. The hint of a smile curved her mouth when Rafe led his accountant onto the dance floor.

"It's all those old-world values and the benefit of a formal upbringing," Joe said, accustomed to hearing women comment on Rafe's perfect mannerisms and charm.

Unlike Rafe, who'd traveled extensively and received only the best education money could buy, Joe's background consisted of surviving the tough streets of the Irish neighborhood in Hell's Kitchen and developing a killer pitching arm to compensate for his little-better-than-average grades. Several top schools had offered him full sports scholarships, but even though he'd had no intentions of becoming a professional baseball player, he'd taken his mom's advice and went with the first Ivy League school to offer him a free ride. While the college dorm had been a major upgrade from the cramped apartment over the bakery where his mom had worked until the day she retired and relocated to Florida, Rafe had ignored his privileged background and the two of them had ended up dorm-mates their freshman year. They'd been as close as brothers ever since.

"And what kind of upbringing did you have?" She tapped her finger on the rim of her glass. "Joe, was it?" she added as if an afterthought.

Go ahead and play your game, sweetheart. Just don't expect to win. "Modest in comparison," he told her. "You?"

She shrugged a slim shoulder. The movement caused her gold dress to shimmer, drawing his attention to the curve of her breasts beneath the metallic fabric. "Nothing out of the ordinary." The sharp edge to her voice said otherwise, hiking his curiosity about the woman he hadn't been able to forget. "So," she said before taking a sip of champagne. "You in town long?"

Guilt pierced him at her subtle jab. "I live in the city now. Or I will just as soon as my apartment is ready." Until Rafe's mother had insisted he move into the mansion a month ago, he'd been living in a moderately priced hotel since his return to New York while searching for a place of his own.

"Apartment?" she questioned. "As in a permanent residence?" At his nod, she added, "How odd."

"How so?" He bit back a smile and braced himself for the next jab.

She shrugged again. "You don't strike me as the kind of person to stay in one place for very long." The comment might have come off as careless if it hadn't been for the brief glimpse of hurt in her eyes. "Now if you'll please excuse me, I made a promise to someone, and I make it a habit to always keep my word."

He caught her hand before she had a chance to escape him again. He deserved her coolness. Hell, he even expected all those slicing passive-aggressive barbs. Coming right out and apologizing to her would probably be what a smart guy would do in the same situation, but when it came to Natalie, he easily admitted to being a first-class fool. Besides, he liked her sharp edges and couldn't help being curious as to exactly how far she planned to take this I-don't-know-you routine.

"Dance with me."

She glanced almost frantically over her shoulder. Looking for someone to rescue her? "I can't." Panic bordered her voice.

With her hand still clasped in his, he narrowed the distance between them. "Sure you can," he said quietly. He lifted his free hand and fingered the pair of gold plumes on the side of her mask. "What's one dance at midnight between old friends?"

3

THEY WEREN'T OLD FRIENDS. They weren't even old lovers, although there was little doubt in Natalie's mind they most certainly would be before dawn. And under no circumstances would she give Joe the opportunity to hurt her again.

She looked up at him, his gray-silver eyes beneath the mask filled with hopeful patience as he waited expectantly for her answer. She let out a breath. "Considering we've only just met," she said, feeling about as truthful as a used-car salesman, "I wouldn't exactly call us old friends."

The lips she had a sudden urge to taste tipped upward with the barest hint of a smile. "One dance." His velvety voice did a number on her determination to keep up the charade. "Because it's New Year's Eve," he coaxed, his smile deepening a fraction.

"Just one," she agreed. As much as she might have liked, she simply didn't possess enough willpower to say no to that cocky half grin two degrees shy of wicked.

He may have only suggested a few turns around the dance floor rather than slipping away somewhere private for something a whole lot more interesting, but since she'd had a brief taste of what making love to Joe could be like, that's exactly where her deprived libido took her. After practically living like a nun, she was more than ready for a little cha-cha beneath the sheets. Besides, she reasoned, if all went as planned, she'd be scratching two goals off her list tonight: satisfy the sadly ignored needs of her body and exact a little payback in the process. A real two-for-one deal.

She stifled a smile. Arianne would be so impressed by her bargaining skills.

The hint of a dimple, half hidden behind his mask, winked at her when he smiled. With their fingers laced together, palm to palm, he led her onto the dance floor. As the band started a slow, sultry jazz tune, she glanced around and spied Isabel heading toward the ornate staircase with a man wearing a gold Venetian lion's mask.

One guess where they're headed. A brief stab of envy pierced Natalie. Oh how she wished she possessed her friend's ability to do what she wanted, when she wanted and with whomever she chose. Natalie might've talked a big game in front of Isabel earlier, but deep down, absolute terror gripped her that her plan would backfire and she'd end up nursing a wounded ego—again.

No, she thought with renewed determination as Joe eased her into his arms. He could only wound her pride if she let him, and she did not intend to allow him anywhere near her emotional boundaries. For once in her love life, she planned to live for the moment. Now there was a motto she could get used to. Damn it, she *would* be impulsive without getting burned.

His big, warm hand glanced down her back to rest at the base of her spine as he drew her close. Sensation rippled beneath her skin where he touched, sending spirals of warmth through her limbs. She could literally count the days since she'd felt anything remotely sexual, and she welcomed the first stirring of honest-to-goodness arousal. In fact, she wanted more. A whole lot more.

Joe kept her left hand clasped in his, holding their

joined hands between their bodies. With her gold bag clasped firmly in her other hand, she lightly rested her wrist over his wide shoulder. She tried to think of something witty and carefree to say, but her mind went blank. Maybe she should just blurt out that she wanted to have hot, sweaty, mindless sex. That ought to melt a polar ice cap or two.

"Natalie?"

The odd note in his voice had her spine stiffening. She looked up and nearly cringed at the guilt filling his eyes.

"I want to apo—"

She quickly tugged her hand from his and placed her finger over his lips. If he said he was sorry for taking off on her last year, she wasn't certain she could continue with her flimsy charade. So long as she kept the illusion alive, regardless of how much they both knew otherwise, she held the power to keep him from crossing the invisible line in her sandbox.

"Don't say anything," she told him. "This is New Year's Eve. It's a time to explore new and exciting possibilities."

He searched what he could see of her face, his gaze intent. "As opposed to righting old wrongs?"

"Why? To ease a guilty conscience?" She hadn't meant to sound so bitter.

"No." Regret laced his voice. "To explain."

"What's the point?" She lifted one shoulder slightly in the kind of careless shrug she'd seen Isabel perform countless times. "Especially if it changes nothing."

"I disagree. An explanation can provide valuable facts."

"Maybe," she said airily, ignoring the twinge of hope attempting to nudge her romantic notions out from under dead bolt and key. Could he really be sorry for pulling a

Houdini on her, or was he hoping to lure her into bed? A man would say just about anything if he thought it increased his chances of having sex. She wasn't about to enlighten him quite yet that tonight was a sure thing. Why ruin a potentially interesting seduction?

"Or maybe not," she added in the same casual tone. "But I'd prefer to concentrate on the present rather than waste time with things that never mattered in the first place."

She looked away and inched closer, effectively putting an end to the discussion. The problem with being a romantic meant she didn't have it in her to hold a grudge for very long. Tonight she wanted her grudges, if only for the false sense of security they gave her. She needed an edge; something to protect herself from believing the potential prince holding her in his arms wasn't a frog after all.

She pushed unwanted fairy-tale endings from her mind, determined to concentrate on the moment, like breathing in his warm, tangy scent. He smelled fresh, like soap and citrus, and more intoxicating than the champagne she'd been drinking like water since her arrival at the party.

With the midnight hour approaching, more couples filled the dance floor, forcing her closer to Joe. Her breasts brushed against his chest. The slight pressure he applied to her back told her he'd definitely been paying attention. Her nipples puckered tight and rasped enticingly against the silk lining of her dress. The gold-beaded thong she wore teased her, and she instantly imagined him caressing her intimately. Arousal filled her, then settled low in the pit of her belly. Dampness collected between her legs before the next downbeat of the music.

She suspected her reaction stemmed from going too

long without sex, but she still marveled at the delicious, insistent pulsing need. Warmth filled her, making her tight and so overly sensitive she felt the length of each of his fingers pressed against her back like a brand on her skin. Even the way his breath fanned her temple as they danced made her hot.

She wanted him. The attraction between them defied logic, but she refused to care. So what if they were virtual strangers who'd shared one sexy encounter a year ago? Okay, so maybe she had foolishly believed she'd fallen in love at first sight. She'd grown since then and would not be making the same mistake twice. All that mattered was the present, and that she'd be ringing in the New Year as a sated woman. And the sooner the better.

TEN.

Nine.

Joe struggled to maintain an even flow of breath when Natalie tipped her head back to look into his eyes. Desire brightened her gaze, leaving him with little room for doubt as to where this night was headed. But not until he made amends.

He'd been raised by a single mother who'd taught him to always treat women with respect. What he'd pulled on Natalie last year hardly qualified. Sure, he hadn't been given a choice, but that didn't excuse the disrespect he'd shown her.

Until tonight, his thoughts of her were filled with lusty images of what could've been. Since seeing her again, guilt ate at him. The sweet sensuality he remembered had changed. The sexiness was still more than evident, but he sensed a cynicism about her now. Whether or not she was merely putting on another act to shield herself from being hurt or if the hardened edge was legit, he couldn't say. Either way, he blamed himself.

Eight.

More guests hurried into the ballroom for the count-down. The crush of people brought them even closer together. With her body plastered firmly against his, he felt every curve.

Seven.

He kept his arms around her, unwilling to release her and risk losing her in the throng of revelers. The warmth of her body fueled the slow, simmering heat that had need clawing hard in his gut.

Six.

Five.

She held his gaze as she moistened her plump bottom lip with the tip of her tongue. His good intentions evaporated like steam rising from the boiler room on his last ship.

Four.

Three.

Two.

He couldn't wait the last second to taste her fantasy-inspiring mouth. "Happy New Year, Natalie," he said, then dipped his head to capture her lips.

One.

His tongue swept urgently past her lips into her hot, moist mouth. His libido exploded. Around them, the cha-otic shouts and cheers of the other guests faded into "Auld Lang Syne." She deepened the kiss, her tongue teasing and mating impatiently with his. She thrust and retreated, encouraging his hopes of having her beneath him before the night ended.

She shifted in his arms and rocked her hips, pressing her sex against his thigh. He groaned into her mouth. His cock throbbed painfully in the confines of his tux when she repeated the movement. The images he'd been plagued with the past year came back to haunt him, only more colorful and vivid. He could practically see and feel Natalie's delicate hands smoothing over his torso. Her fingernails raking his back as he thrust into her moist sheath. Her pink glossy lips poised over the head of his cock as her tongue lapped slowly over the dewy tip.

An odd sensation like hard, smooth pebbles, pressed against his thigh. He ended the kiss to look down at her questioningly. "What was that?" He sounded out of breath, as if he'd just climbed K2 in record time.

A slow, teasing smile turned up the corners of her mouth. "A very special thong."

That explained the lack of panty lines he'd been considering earlier. "Why special?"

She touched the tip of her tongue to the center of her bottom lip as she pressed against him again, then applied pressure to the back of his neck. He lowered his head and she whispered hotly in his ear. "A gold beaded thong."

Just the thought of her tender backside cupping the thong, of the string of those round gold beads teasing and rubbing against her slick center as she throbbed and swelled in anticipation of his touch, of his mouth, had his libido redlining. His hands shook as he reached up to cup her face in his palms. "Show me."

Her smile deepened as she took a step back. She laughed, the sound filled with sinful promise. "Later. Dance with me."

"Take off your mask." The words were more an order than a request. He wanted her to take off her clothes, but considering they were in the middle of a crowded ballroom, he'd save that for later.

"Maybe I prefer a little mystery tonight."

Screw mystery. He wanted to know all of her secrets.

She turned to walk away, but he snagged her hand before she could escape into the crowd. Gently, he urged her back around to face him. "What about tomorrow?" he asked. *What about the rest of your life?*

The blue of her eyes deepened as she closed in on him. Her breasts pressed enticingly against his chest, her nipples beading into hard little peaks waiting for his touch. "I'm not thinking that far ahead."

"How far ahead are you thinking?" He had more than enough ideas on that score to satisfy them both.

She stared up at him for a moment before she slowly reached up to unfasten the clasp holding her gold-sequined mask in place. With great care, she removed it, revealing a sensually wicked expression on her exquisite face. "About as far as the closest bed."

4

As far as Natalie was concerned, outright brazen behavior definitely had its perks. It was liberating, for one, but even more exhilarating was the total sensual power she had quickly discovered she held over Joe. With one crook of her finger, the man would follow her anywhere. And she was loving every second of it.

Of course, she wasn't immune to him, either, and was more than ready to start playing cavewoman by dragging his ass upstairs to have her way with him. Repeatedly.

She let out a quiet sigh, rested her head against his shoulder and closed her eyes. Their bodies were perfectly in tune as they swayed gently to the soft, romantic music, filling her with a sense of contentment. Beneath the jacket of his tux, her fingers strummed the granite-hard muscle along his back.

The song ended just as someone tapped her on the shoulder. With more reluctance than she imagined possible, she pulled back, instantly missing the direct contact of Joe's body against hers.

She turned to find Arianne, her pale Scandinavian skin high with color. "Listen, I've got a headache," Arianne told her, the misery in her voice matching the despair in her eyes. "I think I'll grab a cab home now."

"Everything okay?" Natalie asked, concerned. Arianne had already been dealt one emotional blow today thanks to a late-delivered Christmas card from her ex-boyfriend, complete with a photograph of his new family. She looked as if she'd just been handed another. Did something happen with Rafe? Natalie wondered. Although Arianne had yet to admit it, Natalie and Isabel suspected their friend's interest extended beyond Rafe's debits and credits.

Natalie knew Arianne well enough to recognize a brittle smile when she saw one. "Yes, of course," Arianne said, sounding a little too fragile to quell Natalie's concern. "I'll tell you everything tomorrow at Isabel's."

She'd been so wrapped up in her plans for Joe, she nearly forgot about their traditional brunch at Isabel's loft on New Year's Day, and that she was supposed to bring the fresh bagels. Not a good sign for a woman out to even the score and rediscovering her sexual independence in the bargain.

"Tell Isabel goodbye for me when she surfaces," Arianne said. "And Happy New Year."

Natalie gave her friend a hug. "Same to you," she said. She caught sight of Rafe nodding absently while a new hotshot clothing designer spoke animatedly with his hands. Rafe frowned deeply at Arianne as she headed toward the exit without so much as looking in his direction.

Interesting, Natalie thought, turning back to Joe. At least she'd have something to talk about with her friends tomorrow besides counting Isabel's conquests for the night.

"Let's get out of here," Joe said suddenly.

She looked up at him, and her heart started thumping. He'd been mysteriously handsome hidden behind his mask. Without the black leather shielding so much of his face, Joe Sebastian was one sexy dude, hands down. The black-as-onyx hair, soft gray eyes and strong square jaw were already a major turn-on for her, but the sheer perfection of his straight patrician nose combined with high cheekbones seemingly chiseled from marble made her knees weak just looking at him. He had the sort of lightly polished but still rough enough around the edges appeal that young and hungry fashion photographers clamored to have in their portfolios.

"Excuse me?" she stalled. Her once crystal-clear vision suddenly became shadowed by indecision. Yes, she wanted him. And she desperately needed to deep-six her ridiculous sexual sabbatical. So why on earth was she hesitating?

"Trust me, Natalie."

She hated that he apparently possessed the ability to read her mind. But trust him? How could she when she barely trusted herself not to do something stupid, like fall for him all over again?

She could do this, she thought firmly. She could be the kind of woman that made love to a man then walked away afterward without her emotions cluttering the issue. No, she corrected, not make love. Sex. *Only* sex. The fabulous, mind-blowing, sweaty kind. All she wanted was a piece of ass, and the one hugged quite nicely in Armani would do perfectly.

Get laid and move on—no regrets.

"Let's go," she said, before her conscience rallied in an attempt to change her mind.

Screw the consequences, she reminded herself.

She took his hand and led him away from the ballroom toward the elegantly carved, winding staircase that would take them to the upper floors of the mansion. She remembered the alcove they'd slipped away to last year to share a bottle of champagne and headed in that direction.

"This way," Joe said when they reached the landing.

He guided her away from the alcove with private chaise lounges and high-priced works of art, leading her down a thick-carpeted corridor to another hallway until he finally came to a halt in front of a heavy wood door in the private area of the residence.

She admired the elegant wallpaper and the intricately carved moldings. Her entire apartment would fit inside the width of the corridor, with room to spare. "I don't think we're supposed to be here."

His hand rested on the antique-brass knob. "I'm a guest, remember?"

"Hmm," she murmured. "Friend of the family?" She couldn't help but be mildly impressed. Her acquaintance with Rafe was strictly professional, as was Isabel's now that Monticello Shoes had licensed some of her fabric designs. Arianne's association with Rafe might appear professional, but after what Natalie had witnessed tonight as Arianne was leaving, she had her suspicions on that score.

"Rafe and I went to college together," he said, swinging the door open for her.

Harvard MBAs didn't come cheap and that put Joe Sebastian way out of her league. Her current address might be just off Park Avenue, but once upon a time it'd been the wrong side of town. Girls from trailer parks with drunken fathers weren't allowed to play in the Ivory Tower. Just as well, she mused as she walked past him into the bedroom. Especially if their social differences helped in keeping her from confusing forever fantasies with one-night-stand realities.

She'd expected a standard run-of-the-mill mansion-esque bedroom, and she wasn't disappointed by any stretch of the imagination. A low-burning fire flickered in the imposing marble fireplace, which dominated close to half of one wall. Probably imported from Italy, she thought. She crossed the thick sapphire-colored carpet to inspect the neoclassical painting above the mantel. The piece wasn't one she instantly recognized, but she bet the painting was one hundred percent authentic early Renaissance.

She turned to face Joe as he closed and locked the door, sealing them in absolute privacy. "Didn't you say you had an apartment in the city?"

"I've been away for a while," he said. "My place won't be ready for at least another week, so Lucia insisted I stay here in the meantime."

"Oh?" She smoothed her hand along the wood trim on the back of the tapestry love seat positioned across from a pair of matching wing chairs. "And how long have you been here?" she asked, admiring an antique tea table beside the love seat.

He shrugged out of his tuxedo jacket and walked toward the rear of the bedroom, then stopped beside a monstrous carved four-poster bed worthy of Augustus Caesar himself, complete with sapphire velvet draperies and gold corded ties.

She circled the sofa and moved to stand behind one of the wing chairs, needing something besides electrically charged air sizzling between her and Joe so she could concentrate on calming her racing heart. Now that they were alone, she'd developed a record-setting case of nerves.

He slipped off his cummerbund and tossed the black satin over the end of the chaise in the corner along with his tuxedo jacket. "A couple of months," he said, giving her a meaningful look.

Okay, so maybe that did explain why he hadn't called her the first *ten months* of the year, but it sure as hell didn't justify his ditching her without a word in the first place. Not that it mattered, she amended. She hadn't come upstairs with him to hear lame excuses.

He loosened the bow tie and unfastened the top button of his crisp white shirt. "How long are you going to keep pretending we don't know each other?"

Her vintage Fendi slipped from her fingers and landed on the floor with a dull thud. She didn't bother to make sure the clasp held. Regulating the increased rate of her breathing took every ounce of her concentration.

She gripped the back of the chair so hard her fingers ached. "Who's pretending?" Careless had been her goal. She ended up sounding jittery and high-pitched.

He held her gaze as he moved slowly in her direction. "You are," he said when he reached the love seat.

She forced herself to hold her ground, refusing to run. "I don't know you." Her death grip on the chair tightened. "Champagne? A few kisses? That hardly qualifies as getting to know someone."

Except she *had* known him. At least that's what she'd believed during those blissful, stolen moments a year ago. She'd convinced herself her search for Mr. Right had finally ended. Later she'd realized what she'd actually recognized had been his type—terminal frog.

Her much-needed space evaporated when his long legs ate up the short distance separating them. He stood behind her and slid his hands over her hips. Her pulse fluttered faster than the shutter speed on a top-of-the-line camera.

"We did more than kiss," he reminded her, his breath hot against her ear. If that wasn't enough to have her trembling, he grazed his teeth over her earlobe, then nipped playfully at her nape. She nearly melted into a puddle at his feet.

"I know the curve of your hip," he whispered. His hands traveled with agonizing slowness up her torso. Through the weighty fabric, he palmed her breast. "I know the weight of your breast in my hand. And I know your nipples will pucker when I do this."

To emphasize his point, he brushed his fingers rhythmically over her already sharp, sensitive peaks. "What I don't know, yet," he added, "is how sweet they taste."

The insistent tug of desire had her pressing her bottom against his fly. She felt the hard ridge of his penis along the twist of the beads from her thong as she wiggled her backside. Moisture pooled between her thighs.

He kissed the side of her neck, using his tongue and teeth until her breath caught. "Did you know your eyes turn a brighter shade of blue when you're aroused? Or that you make the sexiest sound deep in your throat as you want more?" His hands left her breasts and slid down her sides until his fingers lightly teased her thighs below the hem of her dress.

She'd be lucky to remember her own name with him touching her. "You obviously have me confused with someone else," she said. Her voice definitely lacked the necessary conviction she'd hoped to convey.

He let out a heavy sigh and moved away from her. "Why do you insist on lying to yourself, Natalie?"

To protect myself from you.

She pushed away from the chair, stooped to pick up her bag and walked toward the bed. Not because she was running away. She just needed to…breathe. "I don't know what you mean."

He followed her. "Your body knows mine. All night it's been acknowledging what you refuse to, and I'd appreciate it if you explained why."

The tenderness in his eyes hit her hard, filling her chest

with a sharp ache. She ignored the threat of her heart opening up to him and managed to produce a saucy grin. "You're just suffering from some weird sense of déjà vu."

"Then why do I feel like I've known you forever?"

The ache reappeared despite her most valiant efforts. "I'm aroused. That's all." She pulled off a caustic laugh. "You could be anyone. Really, it wouldn't make a difference tonight."

His eyes filled with skepticism as he crossed his arms over his chest. The slight lift of one eyebrow said he wasn't buying the line she'd just tried to sell him. Damn. And she'd been hoping there was some truth to there being a sucker born every minute.

"You're aroused," he told her with a touch of arrogance, "because you've been thinking about making love to *me* since last New Year's Eve."

He treaded too close to the truth for her to be completely comfortable. She had thought of him, constantly. She blamed him for her lack of sexual activity. But not, she realized suddenly, because of her hastily made resolution. None of the handful of men she'd dated the past year came close to making her feel the way Joe had with so little effort. All it had taken was a few smoldering gazes, a light brush or two of his hand against hers, the press of a very impressive erection against her backside and she was closer to the edge than she'd been in months—and more than ready to do something about it, too.

"Like I said," she told him, "you obviously have me confused with someone else."

The challenge was obviously too much for him. That confident half smile widened into a full grin. "Wanna bet?"

She simply couldn't refuse. Not if she hoped to win her own battle and finally prove something to herself— that she didn't need to believe herself in love with some guy just to have sex with him.

She tossed her bag on the bed, then reached behind her and tugged down the zipper of her dress. As she lowered her arms, the heavy metallic gold material slid from her body to pool around her feet. She pulled the pins from her hair and shook the long, curly strands loose.

Wearing only the gold-beaded thong, her four-inch Monticellos and a whole lot of false bravado, she looked him dead in the eye. "Go ahead," she taunted him. "Give it your best shot."

5

"I PLAN TO," Joe told her, part threat, part promise. He took the few steps necessary to reach her and pulled her body flush against his, smoothing his hands over her sleek skin. "And this time, I'm not going anywhere."

Her eyes widened slightly, and he sensed her distrust. He hated that he'd done this to her, made her reluctant and suspicious. By morning, he hoped to change all that with an explanation about why he'd left her without a word.

She tossed her head slightly and gave him a manufactured full-of-sass grin. "You talk too much."

"Prefer a man of action and few words, huh?"

Her arched strawberry-blond eyebrows rose a fraction. "Action is all I'm interested in tonight," she said flippantly and pulled out of his embrace.

She turned her back to him and slipped her hand around the bedpost. Resting the other on the tall mattress, she hiked one knee onto the bed, leaving her other foot planted firmly on the floor. "Touch me," she demanded, lifting her backside and opening her legs, offering him the view of a lifetime.

A thin strip of gold material from her thong was tucked enticingly along the seam of her bottom. Round gold beads rubbed her feminine flesh as she moved her hips, both glistening with moisture. His dick throbbed painfully.

When he stood staring at the glorious sight of her so open to him, she lifted her ass a little higher. "Touch me." The repeated demand was warm, husky and too inviting for him to ignore. "Feel how wet," she purred, rolling her hips forward. "And aroused."

Still fully clothed, he moved in to skim his hand over the tender flesh of her derrière. "Because you want me," he told her, bending over to place a kiss on the tiny dimple at the base of her spine.

"Because I'm hot," she countered, bending forward slightly and rolling those curvy hips upward again. "And I do want you—inside me."

He followed the path of the beads with his fingers, pressing and rolling them against her sensitive flesh. Damn, she was wet, and he was ready to come out of his skin. "Only because I've made you that way," he taunted as he eased two fingers deep inside her tight sheath.

She eased out a hiss of breath and pushed back against his hand. He withdrew to tease her with moisture, then rolled the beads back and forth over her swollen clit. A soft moan rose up from inside her when he thrust three fingers deep inside her this time. "You want me, Natalie," he said again, retreating and entering her again and again until her moans coalesced into deep pleasure-filled pleas. "We're here now because it's me that's made you so hot and wet."

She bent farther over the bed and opened wider. The need to taste her overpowered him, but they had all night and he wasn't about to rush their lovemaking now that he finally had her where he'd been imagining her for months. He planned to make her crazy, to the point where anything was possible.

"You want me." He thrust so deep inside her, her

back arched, and she cried out with a long, wild moan of pleasure. He bent over her to nip at her shoulder. "Say it," he demanded.

She tossed her head back, her long red hair curling down her back. "I want you to make me come," she said, then rocked hard against his hand.

He withdrew and ripped the string of beads free. Wrapping the length around two of his fingers, he slowly eased them inside her until she responded with a sharp, desire-filled groan. Her back bowed again and she pushed her ass high and up, giving him full access to her deep, wet core.

His own breath came in short, hard pants as he brought her pleasure. He slightly twisted his hand as he pulled out, over and over. She spread her thighs wider for him, taking him in her sleek heat as far as her body would allow. The roll of her hips became more demanding. Her cries grew louder and more insistent.

"More," she whimpered seductively. Her sheath contracted around his fingers and she rode him harder, faster, taking him fully.

He slid his other hand around her to tease her nipples. She let go of the post and pushed his hand down her torso into her soft, dewy curls. "More," she demanded again, her voice as tight and strained as her body. "Give me more."

With his thumb and forefinger, he gently rolled her swollen clit between his fingers. Her hips bucked wildly beneath his hands, her bottom rising and falling, brushing erotically against his erection still trapped painfully within the confines of his trousers.

Her vaginal muscles clenched tight around him, and she called out his name as she came in a rush. Her hair floated down her slender back in shimmering waves of crimson as she uttered the throatiest, sexiest sound of intense pleasure he'd ever heard while spasm after spasm rolled through her still-trembling body.

"Pretend all you want, sweetheart." He withdrew his fingers and pressed her labia open to tease her throbbing clit by rolling the beads over her tender flesh. "Your body speaks the truth."

"Coincidence," she murmured around another soft groan. She climbed fully onto the bed while keeping her legs open for him to continue stroking her. The only thing missing when she stretched like a languid, contented feline was an accompanying purr.

He gently gripped her hips and guided her onto her back, then carefully pulled her toward the edge of the mattress. Her blue eyes were half-lidded and a satisfied smile curved her mouth as he slid what was left of her thong down her legs. Holding her gaze, he removed her shoes, then set her feet on the mattress and pressed her thighs wide. "I'm going to taste you," he said, inching his fingers slowly toward her damp core.

One of her eyebrows lifted lazily. "Good idea." She opened her arms and reached for him.

Instead of leaning over her to taste her mouth as she'd mistakenly believed, he dropped to his knees and laved her deeply with his tongue.

"Oh, my." He heard her arms flop onto the mattress and felt her back coming off the bed. She sighed.

He took his time, exploring with his tongue and fingers, tasting and stroking, thrusting and suckling the very heat of her until her legs trembled and her entire body was strung tight once again. The release her body craved, he withheld, building the pressure and carrying her closer to the brink with every lap of his tongue, every stroke of his fingers, every graze of his teeth over her ultrasensitive clit. Her hips bucked. Her hands sank into his hair, but she didn't even bother to try to change his course.

"I want you in my mouth." The sexy demand came out a harsh, strained whisper. "I need to taste you."

He debated for about half a second before he left her to remove his clothes. She sat up and held out her hand, her breathing as ragged as his own. Gripping the front of his shirt, she popped every last button with one good yank and discarded the crisp white material by tossing it impatiently to the floor. He made short work of his shoes and socks by the time she had his trousers unfastened. He shucked off his briefs and joined her on the bed.

"Wait," she said when he grabbed for her.

If she changed her mind now, he'd be the one to go insane. His erection pulsed and throbbed painfully. In wanting to drive her past the point of caring, she'd driven him there and beyond with her uninhibited response to their lovemaking.

"I want to look at you," she whispered, her gaze zeroing in on his dick.

He rested on his knees and fisted his hands at his sides as her hands swept across his torso and down to his crotch. Her fingers whispered over his cock and farther down to the underside of his balls. "Poor baby," she cooed, testing the weight of his sac in her small hand. "They're so swollen."

The smile canting her mouth was sexy as hell as she raked him lightly with her nails. He eased out a harsh breath and took hold of her shoulders to draw her close. "I haven't slept with another woman since I met you. You're playing with fire, babe."

The hint of fear and a hefty dose of reluctance returned to her gaze, dimming the brightness of her arousal a full degree. Her body tensed. "Will you burn me, Joe?"

He looked at her steadily. "All night long," he promised, though he knew they were no longer discussing sex, but something much more emotional and frightening for her.

She didn't look entirely convinced, so he dipped his head and kissed her long and hard until her tension slowly eased. Wrapping his arms around her, he hauled her up against him. Still on their knees atop the velvet spread, he slid his hands down her back and pressed his fingers into the flesh of her bottom urging her even closer. With her curves plastered against him, he struggled hard for control.

She ended the deep, exploring kiss long before he was ready, but the moment the tip of her tongue traced his flattened nipple, he lost track of everything but the ends of her fiery hair tickling his erection and her hot, moist mouth sliding down his torso, tasting, nipping and laving.

He stopped her before she could take him into her mouth, but not before her warm breath fanned the tip of his penis in what had to be the most erotic sensation he'd experienced in a decade. She looked up at him quizzically. "I have a better idea," he told her.

If the wicked smile on her face wasn't enough to test his control, the way her tongue slid across that plump bottom lip definitely pushed him that much closer to his limits. With a sweep of his arm, he shoved her purse onto the floor, then settled back on the bed. Taking hold of her hips, he guided her over him, urging her legs open so she straddled his shoulders.

Her breath caught, then expelled in a whoosh when he spread her folds with his fingers then thrust his tongue inside her still-damp core. Her hair brushed his belly, then teased his thighs as she kissed his navel, then snaked her tongue in a heated path down his body and finally

along the length of his cock. She gripped him in her hand
and slowly pumped while he tongued and suckled her clit
until her legs began to tremble.

The heat of her mouth circled his head as her lips
clamped over his length as she took him deep inside with
agonizing slowness. He gripped her hips and licked her,
slowly lapping up the moisture of her need. She released
her hold on him and used only her incredible mouth,
freeing her hands to press his thighs wide so she had
access to every part of him. He trailed his fingers along
the seam of her backside and she moaned with him still
in her mouth. The vibration of sound pushed him closer
to losing control.

He concentrated on bringing her more pleasure in an
attempt to distract himself from the feel of her hands and
mouth on his body. Need raked his gut. His heart
pounded. His cock throbbed inside her mouth as she
pushed him toward fulfillment.

He pushed back, taking her gently into an exploration
of wicked, exotic delights. Her response was wild as she
flew apart and came hard in his mouth. Her lusty cries
from the volcanic force of her orgasm pushed him too
far and too fast for him to regain control. His body
strained and he attempted to urge her away, but she continued to expertly bring him pleasure with her lips,
tongue and the suction of her mouth until his body shook
and he came in a hot, molten rush.

When he had nothing left to give her, she twisted
around and slid her body along the length of his, stopping
when she cupped his face in her soft, delicate palms.
"That was some fire," she said, sounding sleepy and
satisfied. She ducked her head and nibbled his chin, then
suckled the base of his throat.

He chuckled. "Careful. There could still be embers

smoldering.'' With her lying across him, he carefully maneuvered them beneath the covers to ward off the sudden chill in the room as their sweat-slicked bodies cooled.

With a lazy smile on her lips, she wiggled purposefully against him. ''I hear they can flare up without notice and cause all sorts of trouble.''

He hugged her close and she sighed with contentment before lowering her head to his chest. ''Sounds dangerous.''

''Don't worry,'' she murmured. ''I'll protect you.''

Her soft, even breathing signaled she'd fallen asleep before he could summon a reply. As he started to doze, he tightened his hold on Natalie, realizing for the first time since returning to New York, he finally felt as if he'd come home.

6

THE SOFT CLICK of the door jarred Natalie awake. She opened her eyes and blinked several times, momentarily confused by the opulent, unfamiliar surroundings. No way was she tucked inside her sofa bed in her minuscule apartment.

"I woke you."

The sound of Joe's quiet voice made her smile. She turned over, keeping the sleek Egyptian cotton sheet tucked around her, not sure what she was supposed to do now. Walking away before she ended up getting hurt made the most sense. Too bad the stirring need in her belly kept her flat on her back.

She summoned up her sauciest grin. "Now that you've got my attention, what are we going to do about it?"

He chuckled and handed her a bottle of icy cold water before he slipped out of his trousers, giving her ample time to drool over the sight of his nude body. "I'm sure we can find something entertaining to pass the time."

Armani might enhance his incredible physique, but only a stellar gene pool could've created such sheer perfection. He was all wide shoulders, with a tapered waist, lean hips and powerful legs. And he was hers—for the moment.

He slid into the bed beside her and hauled her up against his side. After a much-needed drink of cool water, she handed him the bottle, then smoothed her hand down his chest. "A few things come to mind," she murmured, placing a string of kisses over his torso.

The sharp intake of breath could've been his or hers. She couldn't say and really didn't care so long as he stoked the fire already starting to simmer between them into a full-fledged inferno. Would she ever get enough of this man? She didn't think so, but only this night was allowed. Anything more and she knew she'd never recover a second time.

His hands settled on her shoulders and he very gently urged her away from him. "Let's talk."

She frowned. Talk? What was wrong with him? Men didn't *talk* after having sex. They were supposed to want *more* sex, or go guzzle beer and watch sports on TV. Or in her father's case, go rebuild a carburetor on the kitchen table in a barely habitable mobile home, while she hid out in her room to avoid witnessing another messy scene with the latest barfly that had followed him home. She suppressed a shudder.

She shut the door on a past she'd never completely forget no matter how far away from Shitsville, U.S.A. she'd come. Folding her arms across Joe's stomach, she flashed him another wicked smile. "We could discuss how you're going to make me come again."

His eyes darkened considerably. A very good sign. "Why don't you tell me something about yourself besides your last name?"

Not exactly what she wanted to hear. "There's not much to tell," she said. Correction, there wasn't much she planned to tell him. Only Arianne and Isabel knew the truth, and she trusted them with her life. Literally, she mused, because if anyone ever found out that Natalie Trent was really just a poor kid from the trailer park on the wrong side of town, all the doors she'd worked so hard to open would slam in her face. No chichi designer or model would give her the time of day. The only elbows she'd be rubbing would be in the unemployment line. "I live in New York and work as a freelance fashion reporter."

He set the bottled water on the nightstand. "Do you enjoy it?"

"Who wouldn't?" She caught herself before her enthusiasm spilled over. "Clothes, travel," she added with a flippant shrug. "Parties. What's not to like? If a gal chooses to work, it's the perfect job."

Except she didn't choose to work. She wasn't the bored blueblood she pretended to be. The only reason she could afford the designer originals she'd dreamed of owning was that the magazines she'd pored over as a kid now paid her top dollar for her articles. Deep discounts and designer generosity kept her in the latest fashions. The magazines paid for her trips to Paris and Italy to cover fashion shows and previews. Invitations to all the right parties and events came her way because the socialites and celebrities liked to see their name in print. She moved in a world where people would look down their nose jobs at her if they ever found out she wasn't one of them. She'd done her share of slinging hash and sitting behind a desk all day pushing paper for peanuts to know she could never go back, either.

"What do you do?" she asked before she could stop herself. She wasn't supposed to want to know more about him. Tonight was about getting laid and dulling the edge of her razor-sharp libido. Something she wouldn't mind repeating.

He toyed with the length of her hair, sifting his fingers through the curly ends. "I retired from the Navy two months ago. Now I do investigations," he said.

Her self-preservation radar went off like a fire alarm. "Investigations?" She strove for a calm she was nowhere near feeling. Telling herself she had no reason to panic was a useless endeavor, especially for a woman with something to hide. "Like background checks, looking for deadbeat dads, that kind of thing?" she asked, grateful her voice didn't betray her. The same couldn't be said for her rapidly accelerating pulse or the fear settling in her chest.

He regarded her for a moment before answering. "Background checks are part of the job," he said. "I—"

"You know," she blurted before he could continue, "why are we wasting time with conversation when there are much more pleasurable pursuits we should be exploring?" In a blatant move intended to distract him, she rose up and straddled his hips. "Like this."

She moved against him, rolling her hips. Thankfully he took the hint and gripped her behind, his fingers biting into her skin as he rose up so they were face-to-face. She wound her legs around him and draped her arms over his shoulders. "Make love to me, Joe," she whispered. "We'll talk later."

Without allowing him an opportunity to argue, she caught his lips and kissed him. Slow. Long. Deep.

The flames instantly ignited, filling her with heat. By the time he shifted their position so she was beneath him with her legs wrapped tightly around his waist, Natalie no longer knew where fantasy ended and reality began, but that didn't stop her from enjoying every second of the tender way Joe made love to her.

She lifted her hips to meet his, taking in every inch of his full, hard length. Supporting his weight with his elbows, he rose above her, dragged his fingers through the hair curling at her temples and brought his mouth down to hers for another hot kiss.

She swept her hands down the sculpted landscape of his back to his buttocks, her fingers pressing into the play of muscle with each slow thrust. She wanted all of him. A fair trade, considering the dark-haired devil had taken the one thing she'd sworn to not give him—her heart.

Unwilling to go there, she willed the thoughts from her mind and concentrated on the exquisite pleasure of their joining. Later, when her consciousness wouldn't be quite so easily distracted, maybe then she'd determine how to protect herself from being hurt by him. Now, all she wanted to think about was the incredible buildup of tantalizing pressure with each steady stroke of his body inside hers.

As if she hadn't just experienced the most mind-blowing orgasms of the century, her desire climbed with lightning speed and quickly spun out of control. Their mating became wild, mindless, almost primal. Just as she was close to the brink of orgasm, Joe slowed the pace.

With her eyes still closed, she ended the kiss and tipped her head back. Her neck arched and her body tightened around him as renewed pleasure coalesced through her once again, building with such fierce intensity his name tore from her lips as she flew apart beneath him. Liquid heat spread through her limbs, but she held him to her, her hips rising to accept all of him as he followed her over the edge into pure bliss.

Once the tremors slowed, he carefully moved off her and pulled her close. Tucked against his side, she laid her head on his chest and clung to him, taking in the sound of his ragged breathing and the pounding of his heart beneath her ear. This one night together would be forever etched upon her memory.

Memories, she thought and snuggled closer. That's all she'd ever have with Joe, she realized, because no matter how she might want more, once he discovered the only thing they really had in common was a zip code, there wasn't a chance in hell she'd ever be more to him than a good time. Guys with Harvard degrees didn't marry girls like her. They used them for as long as the fun lasted. Well, no way would she allow him to trample all over her ego, or her foolish heart, ever again. Once had been enough to last her a lifetime.

Regardless of the cost, she remained determined to stick to her original plan. *Get laid and move on—no regrets.* The no regrets part had her worried.

The minutes ticked by with agonizing slowness as she waited for him to fall asleep again. Assured by his deep, even breathing that he'd done just that, she carefully eased away from him. He frowned in his sleep and rolled to his side, his arm reaching across her vacant pillow.

"I'll be right back," she whispered. Apparently satisfied by her lie, he groaned and seemed to relax. She tiptoed around the bed for her dress and shoes. Her thong was history, so she didn't bother with it as she slipped into her dress, then hunted for her bag. She finally found the Fendi hidden partially beneath the bed. The clasp had opened and she crouched down to scoop up the contents that had spilled onto the carpet.

"Natalie?"

Her hand stilled and her heart thundered in her chest. Squeezing her eyes closed, she stayed down, praying he'd go back to sleep. Maybe she should just behave like an adult, she thought with a hefty dose of disgust. Stand up, thank him for successfully contributing to the end of her sexual sabbatical and walk out the door without a backward glance.

Preferring the coward's way out, as soundlessly as possible, she carefully lifted her head to peer over the edge of the mattress. He slept, although the frown still creased his forehead. Slowly releasing the breath she'd been holding, she hurriedly shoved the contents back inside her gold bag, snagged her shoes and crept out the door as silently as a cat burglar.

In the corridor, she stopped to slip on her shoes and attempted to finger comb her hair into a semblance of decency. No music could be heard from the ballroom downstairs, but she did catch the quiet murmur of conversation as she neared the staircase. At nearly four in the morning, she hadn't expected to find any lingering guests or their host.

Holding her head high, she made her way down the curved staircase, relieved when she spied only the wait staff restoring order to the ballroom. She rushed toward the exit and found her coat and the one remaining signature gold box with this year's gift of coveted Monticellos. After double-checking to make sure that her name was on the box, she shrugged into her long black wool coat, took her new shoes with her and left the mansion.

By the time she reached her apartment, her pulse had returned to a more normal rhythm and she was finally able to breathe again. Without bothering to shrug out of her coat, she carried her new Monticellos into the tiny living room, pressing the play button on her flashing answering machine resting on the end table before she dropped onto the sofa bed.

"Natalie, it's me, Arianne." An edge of nervousness filled Arianne's voice, something Natalie couldn't ever remember hearing before. "Huge emergency," Arianne continued in a rush. "We have to move brunch up to eleven."

She considered dialing Arianne, but after a glance at the clock on the DVD player, she quickly dispelled that notion. At four in the morning, Arianne would be sound asleep. Isabel would probably be up, if she was even home, but Natalie needed sympathy, not I-told-you-so's. The answering machine clicked off. Natalie wished she could turn off her emotions as easily.

Refusing to think another minute about anything other than the new Monticellos, Natalie carefully removed the lid with a reverence that would have Isabel rolling her eyes. She peeled back the monogrammed tissue paper to reveal an awe-inspiring pair of black linen mules with a floral design made from fuchsia and lime-green rhinestones across the vamp. She lifted one from the box. Two-inch heels? *Sensible* low heels? For her?

She frowned. Not that the shoes weren't stunning, and she knew they retailed close to five hundred dollars, but what on earth was Rafe thinking? Her in low-heeled shoes? She was a definite skyscraper-kind-of-shoe gal, and Rafe Monticello made a point of knowing the preference of each of his guests at the annual New Year's Eve celebration.

Oh, well, she thought with a shrug and tried them on anyway. They would look fabulous with her black Dana Buchman suit and lime-colored silk Dolce & Gabbana sequined tank. She admired the shoes. As she expected, a perfect fit.

Just like Joe.

She blew out a stream of breath. So what was she supposed to do now? she wondered, slipping the shoes inside the complimentary gold Monticello monogrammed dust bag before returning them to the box. Her plan had worked like a dream. She'd most definitely gotten what she'd wanted because there wasn't an ounce of sexual frustration left in her entire body. Even her pinkie toe was relaxed. She'd managed to walk away without a single word, too, just as he'd done to her last year, classifying the payback part of her plan a huge success.

Unfortunately, the no-regrets aspect was giving her the most trouble. In her determination not to give her heart away, she'd gravely miscalculated, because it was impossible to give something away that had already been stolen from her—three hundred and sixty-five days ago to be exact.

WAKING UP ALONE hardly surprised Joe any more than the sharp sting of disappointment that Natalie had snuck out in the early-morning hours without so much as a goodbye. He'd been so certain he'd finally gained her trust. In some ways he had, if the way she responded to him counted for anything. But apparently not where it mattered most.

He was finally free of his obligations to the Navy. The escrow on his apartment had already closed and once the painters were finished, he'd be moved in by the end of the week. The job with the S.E.C. required minimal travel, but never anything that forced him into absolute silence about his whereabouts. He had nothing but time, and he'd gladly put in as much as necessary to convince Natalie he wouldn't be running out on her again.

He reached across the bed for his cell phone resting on the far nightstand, his intent to check with directory assistance to see if Natalie's number was listed. His fingers brushed against the black plastic casing, spinning the phone so it slid off the polished wood to the floor with a clatter. With a muffled curse, he swung his legs over the side of the bed and walked around to the other side to retrieve the cell phone. A few more muttered curses followed as he had to stoop to look under the bed for the phone.

Along with his cell phone he found a tube of pink lipstick, her gold satin mask and a strip of intact condom packets. They must've fallen out of her purse when he'd pushed it off the bed. Either she hadn't realized or she'd been in too much of a hurry to get away from him to care.

With a flick, he tossed the items onto the bed. He supposed her running out on him was no less than he deserved, but she hadn't given him an opportunity to apologize or explain. He'd tried, and she'd very effectively distracted him. His plan had been to deal with it in the morning, but once more, she hadn't even given him a chance. Instead, she'd served up a dose of his own behavior, and he didn't like it much, either.

He glanced down at the condom packets and wondered if he'd been set up. If he had, he'd been a willing victim and had played right into her skillful hands.

No, he thought, despite feeling the hard nudge of irritation. His pride might have taken a hit that she hadn't wanted to wake up beside him after the night they'd shared, but he didn't believe for a second she'd known he'd be at the party. Her reaction when she'd first seen him had been too genuine. Although he didn't doubt that somewhere along the way, she'd hatched a scheme to give back as good as she got. Of that much he was dead certain. Why else would she have worked so hard to pretend they'd never met when they both knew otherwise?

"Mission accomplished, babe," he muttered. He shoved his hand roughly through his hair. So now what was he supposed to do? Ignore the fact that she'd gotten under his skin? Now that he'd made love to her, forgetting her would be all but impossible.

He let out a sigh and strode into the bathroom for a hot shower. As far as options, he had one, move heaven and earth to find her and explain so they could hopefully move on and see if they had a chance at a relationship. For the first time in a very long time, doubt filled him. If he used her refusal to listen to him last night as a gauge, he honestly didn't know if he'd be able to convince her he at least deserved a shot at making her happy. He might not like it much, but he couldn't ignore the truth—that all he really knew about Natalie could be summed up in a single word—*sex*.

7

NATALIE OPENLY CRINGED as Isabel whacked the radiator for more heat. She didn't know which hurt worse, her pounding head from the champagne she'd guzzled all night as if it were nothing more potent than fruit juice, or the ache deep in her chest where her heart had once been located.

Arianne pulled the chenille throw from the back of Isabel's ratty sofa. "You're not looking so good, Nat," she said, wrapping the throw around her shoulders to ward off the chill in the spacious loft. "A little too much to drink last night?"

Natalie wasn't fooled by Arianne's gentle smile. The woman could sniff out a story better than half the fashion reporters Natalie worked with on a daily basis. "A little too much something-something," she muttered, borrowing Isabel's phrase. She took the blanket Arianne handed her.

Since Isabel shooed them out of her makeshift kitchen, Natalie and Arianne were currently alone, if anyone could really be alone in a wide-open loft like the one Isabel cherished. "You've been in love before," Natalie said, keeping her voice low to avoid a well-meaning confrontation with Isabel. "How did you know it was real?"

Arianne's smile turned wistful. "Considering how that relationship turned out, I might not be the best person to answer your question."

Natalie wrapped her fingers around her coffee mug for added warmth. "But you ended the engagement," she reminded Arianne. She glanced over her shoulder to make certain Isabel was still otherwise occupied. "Was it because you knew you weren't in love with him?"

"Charlie relocated, remember?"

Natalie expelled a frustrated sigh. "I don't buy that. If you'd honestly been in love with the guy, you can't tell me you'd have given up your apartment so fast. Isabel and I would be sending you e-mails this morning with the details of the party last night instead of..." she looked over her shoulder again and shouted "...waiting on mimosas."

"Don't get your thong in a twist," Isabel retorted. "I'm working on it." She muttered something more under her breath, but all Natalie caught were the words *impatient little witch* intentionally spoken loud enough for her to hear.

Natalie managed a quiet chuckle as Arianne's eyebrows rose a notch before she slipped a pale blond strand of hair behind her ear. She gave Natalie a level stare over the rim of her coffee mug. "Why so curious about ancient history all of a sudden?"

"I had sex with Joe last night," she said, once again taking care to keep her voice low.

Arianne hardly looked surprised as she regarded her carefully. "And now you regret that decision?"

Natalie mistakenly shook her head, sending off a fresh round of pounding. She winced and rubbed her temples. "I'm just trying to figure out why."

"Why you made love to him?" Arianne asked, then took a sip of her coffee.

"Not exactly. More like why I *could* make love to him." Natalie let out another sigh and leaned forward to set her mug on the rough-hewn marble slab that served as Isabel's coffee table. "Since last year when we made our resolutions, I haven't felt the least bit aroused by any of the guys I've dated all year. It's as if I couldn't connect on that level, you know."

Arianne nodded and burrowed deeper within the chenille throw.

"But last night with Joe...it was..." Natalie searched for the right word. "Explosive," she admitted. "There's never been anything like it for me."

Arianne considered her for a moment. "Maybe the reason you weren't able to connect, as you say, with any of those other guys is because your heart already belonged to someone else?"

Natalie winced again, and this time not from the pain in her head, but the one in her chest. "I was afraid you were going to say that."

"Well," Arianne said with a quick lift of one shoulder. "Maybe he just kept it for himself."

Natalie smiled. "That has to be the most illogical thing I've ever heard you say."

Arianne was nothing if not perfectly logical at all times. She kept her checkbook balanced to the penny, her credit cards never carried a balance from month to month and she already had an impressive stock portfolio, something she'd gently nagged Natalie into starting for herself. The money she placed into her own investment account had cut dramatically into her monthly clothing and shoe budget, but even she had to admit that she'd gotten used to the idea of long-term security.

"So what are you going to do now?" Arianne asked her.

Natalie hadn't a clue. She could wait around for Joe to call, and then when he didn't, she'd be crushed. Or she could be the one to make the next move, but if he blew her off, then she'd still end up with a flattened ego. Maybe she just needed to get over herself, move on and screw regrets.

"Oh," Natalie said suddenly, relieved to have a change in topic. "Rafe has finally agreed to an exclusive interview and said he'll let me have a preview of the upcoming fall line they'll be introducing in the spring. I guess I have you to thank."

"Me?" Arianne's light blond eyebrows pulled down in a frown. "I didn't do anything."

Natalie gave her a skeptical look. "You didn't put a good word in his ear on my behalf?"

"No, I did not," Arianne told her. "You need to have some faith in yourself, Nat."

Isabel walked into the living room area cordoned off by lengths of gauzy fabric flowing from the overhead conduits and pipes. She carried an unmatched set of glasses filled with the best hangover antidote Natalie knew to exist—mimosas. "Why does she need faith?" Isabel asked, handing Natalie a glass. "What did you do? Fall in love anyway?"

"No," Natalie said defensively. Isabel's skeptical expression said she wasn't convinced. Natalie stifled another sigh. When would she learn she couldn't keep anything from her two best friends?

"Rafe's giving her an exclusive," Arianne explained. "She doesn't believe she got it based on her own merit."

"Don't be such a weenie, Nat," Isabel scoffed with a wide grin full of pride before heading back into the kitchen.

"I'm supposed to be at the mansion by three o'clock," Natalie said.

"So what's the problem?"

She hated to admit that Isabel was right, but if she couldn't talk to Arianne and Isabel, then who could she talk to? "Joe will probably be there. He's staying at Rafe's until his apartment is ready next week."

"Ahh," Arianne said before taking a sip of her drink. "You're afraid to see him."

Natalie dropped her head back against the threadbare sofa. "This wasn't supposed to be complicated." She went on to explain her plan, which had backfired on her. "I just can't do it. I really tried. I actually had myself convinced I could have sex and walk away, and I did pull it off, except…"

"Except you fell in love with him anyway."

"Yeah. I did," Natalie said miserably. "It doesn't make sense, either, because I really don't even know the guy. I still don't know why he even pulled that Houdini act last year, but that's my fault because he did try to apologize, and I didn't let him. And, to top it off, I can't even tell if what I'm feeling is the real deal. Besides, he's social register and I'm…not."

"I seriously doubt that makes a difference." Arianne reached across the sofa and settled her hand over Natalie's and gave her a reassuring squeeze. "Nat, maybe you've just been in love with him all along."

Natalie was saved from having to respond to Arianne's all-too-knowing statement when Isabel returned with a serving tray laden with the fresh bagels Natalie had remembered to pick up from Balducci's, a variety of cream cheese and a heavenly, aromatic frittata.

"So," Isabel said cheerfully. "That party! Was it amazing, or what?"

As they ate the goodies Isabel had prepared, they chatted about the evening, the shoes Rafe had given them and the most interesting tidbit of all, the news that Ar-

ianne had not only slept with Rafe last night, but she'd
be seeing him again tonight. After Natalie and Isabel had
raided Isabel's thrift-shop wardrobe to arm Arianne with
the appropriate attire guaranteed to sufficiently drive the
man to his knees, Natalie and Arianne shared a cab home.

"Call me after the interview," Arianne told her as she
exited the cab.

"I will," she promised, then waited until Arianne disappeared inside her building. "96 East 77th," she told
the cabbie. "Just off Park." She'd have to go to the interview dressed as she was since she only had enough
time to make it back to her apartment to grab her tape
recorder and the notepad with her list of questions before
heading directly to the Monticello mansion.

She had no idea if she would even see Joe. Her tummy
fluttered with nervousness, all because she worried that
last night hadn't meant as much to him as it did to her.
What was the difference anyway? They were all wrong
for each other. How could she possibly hope to have a
truly intimate relationship with a man when she feared
risking her career? No matter how antiquated her
thoughts, a social class structure *did* exist, especially if
you were the one from the wrong side of the tracks.

Regardless of the outcome, as Isabel had so eloquently
stated, at least she'd gotten herself good and screwed.
Based on the past year, she figured that was as close to
embracing her inner wild woman as she would probably
ever come.

8

FOR WHAT HAD TO BE the hundredth time, Joe reread the phone message from Rafe, which the Monticellos' housekeeper had given him less than two hours ago. He was asking Joe to keep Natalie at the mansion until he returned from a charity auction with his mother. With every reading, Joe's anticipation grew. Natalie would be arriving any second now, and if he had to tie the woman to a chair and gag her so she'd listen to him, he'd do it. He was not about to let her slip away from him again until she heard his explanation and subsequent apology. Whether or not she'd accept it…

Other than a skeleton staff working on the holiday, he was alone since Lucia and Rafe had left long before he'd ventured from his room. On his own, he had too much time to think. To say he was nervous was an understatement.

The ringing of the doorbell had him sprinting to the foyer and nearly colliding with the housekeeper. After a mumbled apology, he bolted for the door and swung it open.

Hot damn, he thought, sweeping his gaze over Natalie. Entirely too sensual for his peace of mind, she easily played hell with his libido. Forget tying her to a chair. Carting her off to the closest bed and making love to her suddenly sounded like a much better way to spend the afternoon.

Beneath her unbuttoned long black wool coat she wore a pair of figure-hugging camouflage pants, lethally high-heeled black leather boots and a short cropped black sweater that clung too enticingly to her full breasts and showed off a strip of skin just below her navel. She wore her hair down, the blondish-red curls gleaming in the winter sunshine. She looked like a fiery goddess sent to drive him to his knees. While he was down there, he'd better start by begging for her forgiveness.

She hitched her big leather bag higher on her shoulder and gave him a cool stare. "I have a three o'clock with Mr. Monticello." As if he were nothing more than a servant paid to do her bidding, she gave him one last dismissive glance before striding into the foyer with her head held high and her back straight. "Tell him Natalie Trent is here to see him, please."

The floral scent of her perfume lingered as she passed, resurrecting memories of their night together. The silky texture of her skin, bared and sleek beneath him. Her gentle moans of pleasure as he slid his body into hers. The way her blue eyes darkened to the color of sapphires when she came apart. Every scent, every sound, every glide of their bodies rushed through his mind. And she had the gall to pretend none of it had ever taken place?

The irritation he'd felt when he'd awakened to find her gone returned, courtesy of her dismissive attitude, slamming into him hard. Without meaning to, he closed the door with a brisk snap, but a morbid sense of satisfaction still filled him when she flinched. At least she wasn't totally immune.

"Rafe's been detained," he said. "He asked that you wait." She followed when he took off for the study, the heels of her boots clicking a brisk pace behind him on the Italian marble tiles. He headed straight for the bar, needing a drink. He needed a lot of drinks to douse the images of Natalie writhing beneath him. Images she'd apparently had little trouble banishing from her mind.

She moved to the leather sofa and sat primly on the edge. "Will Rafe be long?"

Instead of answering her, he poured himself two fingers of scotch, drained the glass in one swig, then poured himself another before turning around to face her. "How long are we going to play this game, Natalie?" he asked, his tone more brusque than he'd planned.

She visibly winced, her who-the-hell-are-you façade slipping. She cleared her throat. Shoring up waning confidence maybe?

"Excuse me?" she asked.

The look he shot her clearly said his patience was wearing thin—which she ignored as she stood to shrug out of her coat.

"I think you heard me."

She laid the heavy wool over the arm of the sofa before tossing a saccharine smile in his direction. "Aw, what's the matter, Joe?" Her earlier dismissal of him faded into her own brand of irritation, complete with a brightness to her eyes he thought completely intoxicating. She hooked her thumbs over the edge of her pockets. "Don't like how it feels when someone vanishes without a word?"

He made a sound somewhere between a laugh and a grunt of self-disgust. At least she was willing to acknowledge their brief past even existed. "No, I don't," he admitted. "Even though I might have deserved it, I still don't like it."

Her eyes narrowed. "Sucks being used, doesn't it?"

"Used?" He understood how she might've felt that

way, but he hoped to dispel the erroneous notion if she'd just let him explain.

"That's right. Used." She crossed her arms and cocked her hip slightly to the side. "For sex. I needed to have sex and you were handy. Was I supposed to leave a hundred-dollar bill on the nightstand? Sorry," she said, narrowing her eyes again. "I'm not quite up on the appropriate protocol when using someone for a quick lay."

He set the glass down hard on the bar, then stalked across the room to stand directly in front of her. "We both know what's really going on here, Natalie, so cut the bullshit. You're pissed at me for taking off last year, so you thought you'd even the score. Fine. You win. I didn't like waking up alone this morning. Satisfied?"

"What makes you think I even care?"

"Oh, come off it," he said with a little too much heat based on the way her eyebrows winged upward. "It doesn't take a genius to figure it out, Nat. What I want to know is why you won't let me explain?"

Her arms fell to her sides. "It doesn't matter." The way her gaze shifted to the floor and her shoulders slumped slightly forward said otherwise. It mattered to her—a lot.

"If that's true, then why are you so hell-bent on making me pay?"

"It really doesn't matter," she said again and turned away. She dropped back to the edge of the sofa and made a huge production out of straightening the already perfectly aligned sleeves of her sweater. "Look, we had a great time. Thank you. You were fabulous. Maybe I'll call you sometime."

If her voice hadn't suddenly taken on a brittle note, he might have believed her cavalier act. Except he wasn't buying what he perceived as a defense mechanism. God, he hated himself for what he'd done to her, even if he hadn't had a choice. Something he was determined she would understand, and hopefully accept.

The need to be close to her drove him to the sofa to sit beside her. Lifting her hand, he laced their fingers together. Even though she refused to look at him, he took it as an encouraging sign when she didn't pull away from his grasp. "Do you remember last night when I told you I had recently retired from the Navy?"

She offered a brisk nod in reply.

"I was in Naval Intelligence, Nat. A SEAL officer. That night I left without saying goodbye, I was called away under Executive Order to extract two Americans from a classified location, which I'm not permitted to discuss even now."

She turned to look at him. When she issued a short bark of laughter, his heart sank. "You expect me to believe you were called away—on New Year's Eve no less—on some mission so top secret you couldn't even tell me you were leaving?" She laughed again and yanked her hand from his grasp. "Score one for originality, because that's the best excuse I've ever heard. And believe me, I've heard plenty."

When she put it that way, the truth did sound rather ludicrous. "It was over two months before I returned stateside," he explained, unwilling to give up all hope. "I didn't even know your last name, where you lived, worked. Nothing. Rafe was out of the country and by the time he returned, I'd been sent overseas again. I've been back since late October and I figured too much time had passed. I'm sorry, Natalie. I wanted to call you. I never meant to hurt you."

She shook her head, her disbelief apparent. "Most guys would've just said, 'Hey babe, sorry. Uh, uh…I lost your number?'" she mocked in a bad imitation baritone. When she finally did cast her eyes his way, all the hurt he'd caused her shone in their brilliance, twisting his conscience and his heart like the sharpness of a blade.

She flew off the sofa suddenly and faced him down, a vision of barely tempered fire that heated his blood. "Exactly how stupid do you think I am?"

"Wh—?"

"What is this?" she demanded, her tone rising a full octave. "Some warped attempt to make me feel guilty for wanting you to feel a little of how I've felt all year? What happened? Your precious ego take a direct hit because I didn't bother to wake you before I left this morning to wax on about how you were the greatest lay I've had in years?"

"Before you sneaked out, you mean." He was hardly furthering his cause to get back onto her good side by sniping at her, but damn it, she'd exhausted his patience. A guy could only take so much browbeating before he snapped a little, no matter how wrong he might have been in the first place.

"What difference does it make? We had sex. It was good." Her gaze turned glacial. "Move on. It's what you do best," she spat at him.

A strong offense was quite often the sign of a desperate defense, or an attempt to hide the truth, and Natalie was doing a bang-up job of doing one or both. He'd stake his life on it.

He stood and approached her. "What are you afraid of, Natalie?" he asked gently.

She crossed her arms and refused to look at him. "Nothing."

God, he hated when women said that. Nothing was *always* something. And the poor schmuck that heard that fateful word would pay dearly until he figured out exactly what he'd done wrong. Well, he knew where he'd screwed up and he'd apologized for it once already. He'd be damned if he'd do it again.

"Nothing, my ass," he argued. "If you weren't afraid, you wouldn't have sneaked out of here like a coward."

She spun around to face him. "Coward?" She gave him one last heated look filled with loathing, then moved to scoop up her coat and bag. "I don't need this."

He was beside her in less than a heartbeat. With his hands on her shoulders, he gently turned her around to face him. "You need me."

"I don't need *any* man," she argued. "I used to think so, but you've cured me of that misconception. Leave me alone, Joe. That should be real easy for you. You've had an entire year to perfect the skill."

"Damn it, Natalie. I said I was sorry. What do you want from me?"

"You really want to know?"

"Yes, I want to know. Give me that much."

"Fine," she shouted back at him. "I want someone who is going to be there in the morning. A guy who isn't going to disappear on me without notice." She let out a long slow breath and gentled her tone. "I want the fairy tale, Joe. The house in the 'burbs with the white picket fence and a minivan parked in the driveway. A big, lazy chocolate Lab that likes to lie by the fireplace. And going to bed every night knowing that when I wake up every day, someone will be there to share every minute with me."

Panic gripped him with icy fingers. He'd left the Navy because deep down he'd believed he would one day want those things, too. Did he have what it took to stick around for the long haul? He'd been on the move for so long, he honestly couldn't state with any amount of certainty that he had it in him to share every minute of what she described. With her or any woman for that matter.

"What's the matter, Joe?" she asked. "Afraid? Feeling a little cowardly?"

"What are you saying?" His voice sounded strangled. As if the proverbial noose in the shape of a pair of matching gold bands had been welded around his neck, cutting off his air supply. "You want forever? Now?"

She made a sound of disgust and shrugged out of his grasp. "Don't be obtuse. Of course not."

"Then what?" He wished she'd explain it to him. Then maybe he could breathe again.

"The idea, Joe. I want to know the *idea* of forever is a real possibility."

She looked at him expectantly, waiting for an answer he didn't know if he could give. He wanted to tell her it was possible, but he couldn't seem to find the right words. Who was he kidding? He could hardly draw breath let alone summon a single word that would placate her.

The anger and heat faded from her eyes, replaced by a sadness he felt clear to the bottom of his nomadic soul. She slung her bag over her shoulder. "Sometimes it's what you don't say that says the most. Goodbye, Joe."

He didn't even try to stop her when she walked out of the study. What could he say that wouldn't be a lie? Considering their history, she deserved better than being dished up a serving of false hope. The eventual slamming of the door moments later held more finality than he wanted to acknowledge, or was sure he could accept.

By the time Rafe showed up less than an hour later, Joe was nursing his third scotch. "Join me for a drink?" he asked his friend.

Rafe strode to the bar and poured himself a bourbon before taking a seat in one of the matching leather chairs across from Joe. "I'd ask what we're celebrating, but you don't look like you're in a party mood."

Joe lifted his glass in mock salute. "Morphine substitute." He downed more scotch. "For the pain of having my nuts served up on a silver platter."

Rafe winced. "Sounds bad. What happened?"

Joe wasn't about to argue. With his elbow resting on the arm of the sofa, he dropped his head against his fingertips and rubbed his throbbing temple. "FUBAR, buddy. Big time."

Rafe propped his foot over his knee. "I take it Natalie was the one doing the carving."

"Woman's great with a knife."

Rafe chuckled and checked his watch. "Where is she, by the way?"

Joe finished off the booze and seriously considered a refill. "Probably still condemning me to hell. Maybe crafting a voodoo doll and driving a railroad spike or two through it for shits and giggles. Cursing the day we met. I don't know," he said with a helpless shrug. "Take your pick. As pissed as she is at me, the options are limitless."

Rafe cleared his throat, but Joe still caught the grin his friend attempted to hide. "What did you do to her?"

Joe let out a weighty sigh. "Before or after I called her a coward because I was ticked that she threw my apology back in my face? Maybe you'd rather hear about how I let her think she wasn't the kind of woman worth waking up to every morning for the rest of my life."

Rafe's hearty laughter made Joe feel worse, which wasn't saying much. He decided a fourth scotch sounded like a good idea and made his way over to the bar. Not bothering to add ice, he just poured.

He didn't think he could have sunk any lower than he had today. He'd hurt her—again—and didn't have the first clue how to make amends for his latest screwup. Considering how he'd already fumbled, he seriously doubted she'd make it easy on him if he dared another attempt.

Joe returned to the sofa. "I figured she'd be ripped about last year, but once I explained to her why I'd left the way I did, she'd be okay with it." He realized how feeble his explanation must've sounded to Natalie, and how faulty his thinking had been. "When that didn't work, I let her think she's not important enough to me. How am I supposed to fix this?" he asked, but he already suspected the answer.

Rafe's knowing grin sank the last nail into the coffin of Joe's last remaining shred of pride.

Joe massaged his throbbing temple again. "This is going to require groveling, isn't it?"

"Across hot coals on your hands and knees," Rafe said. At least his expression held a modicum of sympathy.

Joe set the full glass on the mahogany table and stood. Three glasses of the scotch had dulled his mind enough. He'd need every square inch of his gray matter fully functional if he was going to convince Natalie the idea of forever could exist. He wasn't about to make any long-term promises, but at the very least, she deserved to know she was important to him.

"Where are you going?" Rafe called after him as he headed for the door.

"To find some hot coals."

9

NATALIE KEPT one short step ahead of the deep dark abyss of true despair by first diving inside a bag of macadamia-nut-white-chocolate-chip cookies, then leaping into a supersize bag of BBQ potato chips and a questionable container of sour cream. When those weapons were in danger of losing their power, she went for the hard stuff—a fresh pint of double-chunk fudge ice cream.

Crying until her eyes were puffy beyond recognition for being foolish enough to believe she just might be important enough to a guy like Joe hadn't helped. Neither had ranting and swearing followed by a particularly good mope because she'd let her heart get stomped into the dirt—again! She knew she was in bad shape when the frozen cure-all failed to lighten her spirits.

She let out a sigh and dropped the spoon into the empty ice-cream container. No matter how she looked at the mess she'd once again made of her love life, this time she knew her heart had been shattered so badly it would take years to mend. Maybe by the time she reached eighty she'd feel better.

She had her doubts.

The pain and humiliation inside her ran so deep, she wasn't even sure where it began or how to mend it. She hadn't called Arianne as she'd promised because she didn't want to bring her friend with her on the downer from hell when Arianne was preparing to embark upon the affair of the decade with Rafe Monticello in a few hours. Natalie had weakened though and had tried calling Isabel, but all she'd gotten had been Iz's voice mail, so she'd hung up without leaving a message. Just when she needed a good talking-to to remind her what a fool she'd been, Isabel had blipped off the radar screen.

Natalie turned down the volume on the decorating show she hadn't really been watching for the past hour, brushed cookie crumbs from her favorite pair of pity-me flannel pj's and reached for the phone to try Isabel again. Instead of dialing the voice of sarcastic reason that would give her a good chuckle, she called home.

By the fourth ring she was prepared to hang up, but the gravelly voice caused by a two-pack-a-day habit for the past forty years came on the line. "Yeah?"

"Happy New Year, Dad," she said with forced brightness. She didn't need to close her eyes to see the peeling wallpaper in the cramped bathroom, the faded threadbare rug in the faux-walnut-paneled living room or the smudged grease stains on the counter near the fridge because her father's first stop when he left the garage where he worked as a mechanic was the kitchen for a beer. Those images would remain burned in her mind for all eternity. They were home, and a reminder of how far she'd come.

"I didn't wake you, did I?" What she really meant was he sleeping off another bender?

"Natalie!" Paul Trent said her name cheerfully, if a bit slurred. "How are you, baby girl? The big city treatin' you good?"

"The question is how am I treatin' the big city?" Her father might have been the local drunk in the small hick town where he still lived and served the community as one of the best mechanics in three counties—when he was sober—but she'd never doubted his love for her. They hadn't had much, but they did have each other. Her mother had died when Natalie was a child, but her dad had done the best he knew how, even if his priorities were often skewed.

She hugged the chenille throw tighter around her shoulders and looked over at the little eighteen-inch fake Christmas tree in the corner on the table and was reminded of the one concession her father had never failed to grant her—a real Christmas tree. There hadn't been much by way of presents, but at least he'd kept his promise and remained sober for Christmas.

"That's what I like to hear," he said with a laugh that led into a coughing spasm.

By the time she hung up the phone thirty minutes later, she did feel a mite more pleasant, as her dad was fond of saying. The ache in her heart remained, but her mood had indeed improved.

The abrupt knock on the door momentarily startled her. Probably Arianne, she thought, stopping by to borrow a more sedate outfit because she'd flown into a last-minute panic over that red number she and Isabel had foisted on her. Natalie walked the short distance to the door, mentally running through her wardrobe for something red that would work for Arianne, and opened it to find no one there.

She frowned and stepped back to close the door when she heard a scratching noise, followed by a whimper. Glancing down, she spied a cardboard pet carrier.

She glanced down the hallway to see if the deliverer was there before crouching down and opening the top on the carrier. She couldn't blink back the tears fast enough.

Sitting inside, looking up at her with dark brown eyes was a chocolate Lab puppy, its little head cocked to the side and the floppy ears pert. She swiped at the tears and reached for the pup, cuddling—she checked—*her* to her chest. "This does not mean you're forgiven," she called out, wondering where the jerk was hiding. "No, it doesn't," she murmured to the pup busy nuzzling Natalie's chin. "But it's a good start."

She pulled the carrier inside then leaned against the doorjamb to wait for Joe. Moments later, she heard his footsteps on the stairs. "She's adorable," she told him. What she was going to do with a puppy, especially in her tiny apartment, she wasn't quite sure, but no way was she giving up this warm little ball of fluff. "How did you pull this off?"

Isabel would call her an idiot and read her the riot act for even speaking to Joe after the way he'd treated her. After Arianne calculated the annual cost of owning a dog, at least she'd offer a sympathetic shoulder and a box of tissues while Natalie cried an ocean.

Joe shrugged his wide shoulders and gave her a sheepish grin that hiked up the rate of her pulse a few notches. "I couldn't find any hot coals suitable enough for crawling over on my hands and knees."

"Pity," she said and waved him inside. "I guess you'll show up with a minivan next if I don't let you in."

He winced, then glanced around her tiny apartment, his gaze landing on the empty wrappers and containers littering the end table. When he looked back at her, one sweep of his gaze had him frowning. "You're wearing ridiculously expensive shoes with ratty flannel pajamas."

"Not that it's any of your business, but I'm breaking them in." She hugged the pup tighter to her chest and resisted the urge to slip out of her new black linen mules. "Why are you here, Joe? Come to remind me I'm not good enough? I got the message the first time."

"I never said you weren't good enough." At least he had the decency to appear contrite. "I came to apologize, but I'll probably make a mess of it, so I brought reinforcements," he added with a nod toward the puppy now sound asleep in Natalie's arms.

"Grovel away," she told him, swearing it wouldn't make a bit of difference to her. She'd come up with a new resolution for the year. No more heartbreak. Ever. She'd invest in a good vibrator before she let another man close enough to hurt her again. Especially the one crowding her tiny apartment with his worship-worthy body, no matter how many orgasms he gave her.

He took a step toward her, then hesitated. "I'm sorry, Natalie."

He deserved to be drawn and quartered. Boiled in cheap perfume could be fun, too. She was still angry enough with him for hurting her that she could easily devise a hundred different ways to torture him to her satisfaction, but seeing him hesitant and unsure shook her resolve—hard. And well, he had given her a puppy, something she'd wanted from the time she could walk.

He took another tentative step in her direction. "Do you think you can ever forgive me?"

"I'm through letting you trample my self-esteem, Joe. Go find someone else to treat like dirt."

He let out a rough sigh and jammed his hand through his hair. "I'm sorry," he said again, looking about as miserable as she'd been feeling since leaving the mansion this afternoon. "I'm sorry I hurt you. There isn't anything I can say except that the idea of forever is a possibility. Tell me what I have to do to convince you, and I'll do it."

A fat lump lodged in her throat. "Keep talking," she

whispered, blinking back another round of moisture threatening to blur her vision.

His big, warm hands settled on her shoulders. "I know we don't know each other all that well, but I do know that you're important to me. I can't make you any promises, Natalie. I've been on the move for so long, I really don't know if I can stay in one place longer than a few months." His voice was suspiciously tight and filled with an honesty that touched her and did a real number on soothing her battered heart. He pulled her close and wrapped his arms around her and the puppy. "But there is always a chance for more."

She pressed her lips together to keep her chin from quivering. Damn it, hadn't she cried enough for one day? Apparently not, because the minute he swept his hand down her spine, her emotional floodgates gave way.

He took the sleeping dog from her and carefully placed her back inside the carrier. Natalie slid her arms around Joe's waist and held on tight. With her face burrowed into his soft shirt, she sobbed some more. When there was nothing left but a case of the hiccups, he led her to the sofa bed, handed her a tissue and tucked her close to his side as if he planned to never let her go.

Once her hiccups ebbed, she tilted her head to look up at him. "Before you start believing in possibilities, too, there's something you should know."

He smoothed the back of his hand tenderly down her cheek. "What's that?"

"I'm not some rich chick with a perfect pedigree playing at having a job because I'm bored," she admitted. "The only thing blue about my bloodline is blue collar. I moved to New York after working full-time as a waitress in a truck stop off the Interstate so I could pay my own way through community college. I got my journalism degree and got the hell out, but my dad's still a grease monkey in the hill country of Kentucky where I grew up, and he's not always sober, either.''

He frowned. "What does that have to do with anything?''

"We don't come from the same place,'' she told him. "I'm community college and you're Harvard. You're New York City and I'm still a country girl at heart.''

He smiled and shook his head. "I don't care where you came from, Natalie. The only reason I got into Harvard was because of a ninety-eight-mile-per-hour fastball. My mom worked in a bakery in Hell's Kitchen and we lived upstairs. I can tell you where some of the finest restaurants in New York are only because I worked as a busboy in a few of them in high school.''

She couldn't stop the bubble of laughter from erupting. How could she have been so stupid? "What do we do now?'' she asked him.

"I'm not sure, but I do know I don't want to lose you. Whatever it takes for you to trust me again, just tell me and I'll do it.'' His arm tightened around her and the tension eased from his body. "So, you want to start over again? Maybe I can get it right this time.''

She pulled back to look at him again. "Starting over isn't what has me worried.''

"The endings, huh?''

She nodded. Going through another day like today and she'd be forced to take drastic steps. Like entering a convent. "Could get ugly,'' she said.

Her breath caught at the raw emotion shining in his soft gray eyes. "I'm never going to let you go now that I've found you—again,'' he said.

She climbed over his lap to straddle his hips and wreathe her arms around his neck. "You talk too much.''

"That's right," he said as his eyes turned smoky. "You prefer a man of action over one of words."

"Hmmm," she murmured before brushing her mouth lightly over his. All her life she'd believed in fairy tales, fate and whatever entity she could drum up in search of a happy ending. Whether she and Joe would have that happily-ever-after, she couldn't guess, but something had brought them together, not once, but twice. And perhaps even a third time if she wanted to get technical about the whole thing. Maybe she'd finally have her own happy ending now that her prince promised to not disappear on her again. With odds like that in her favor, who was she to argue?

ENTICING
Carrie Alexander

1

To: IsabelParisi@NYletterbox.com
From: Tom@Gracenotes.biz
Subject: New Year's Eve

Dear Beautilicious: Just a quick note to wish you the happiest of New Years. Are you sure you don't want to bag that fancy-schmancy party you're going to and come to my place instead? We could stay in and snuggle by the fire, just you 'n me and the boob tube broadcasting a gazillion insane New Yorkers crammed into Times Square. The backgammon board is always set up and the corner deli is delivering right up till midnight. Yes, I'm offering lowly pastrami on rye and cream soda in place of unrecognizable hors d'oeuvres and Dom Pérignon. Crazy, perhaps, but just picture it, *ma bella.* You and me face-to-face at last.

Gulp.

No, really. Don't worry. I'm only half the beast you're imagining. If I'm lucky, you might even decide that being lovers and being friends are not mutually exclusive states of being.

No?

Ah, well. One day we *will* meet. Until then, I remain your humble carpenter and devoted beast,

Tom

P.S. If you drink too much of that damn Dom, write the word and I'll be over with the hair of the beast...er, dog.

To: Tom@Gracenotes.biz
From: IsabelParisi@NYletterbox.com
Subject: re: New Year's Eve

Beastly man, don't tempt me! When we started our Napoleon-and-Josephine, Griffin-and-Sabine, Tom-and-Meg correspondence all those months ago, you swore on a stack of the finest Brazilian teak and I on a swatch of French toile du Jouy that we would remain strictly friends. We can't change now.

Please don't be hurt; you know I adore you.

Maybe it's all this ringing out the old year stuff that's making me nostalgic, but I've been thinking back to our beginning. After that first e-mail (how proper and businesslike you were!), I never expected that we'd become not only friends, but best, best, best of online friends. Even if only *you* had the good taste to recognize my brilliance in textile design—before the Monticellos made me a star, tra la, tra la! ;-)

I think it was the first time I saw my fabric on a Grace Notes piece in the window of a Madison Ave showroom (enough with the humble carpenter boo-yah, Tom) that I realized ours was a meeting of the minds unlike any other. We go together, like damask on a settee. And that's exactly why it's better to maintain our separation. I wouldn't have come to treasure you the way I do if I'd had to throw your furry beast butt out of bed The Morning After. You know how I am.

Okay?

Well, I'm off to the masquerade party now, just me and Arianne and Natalie and something-less-than-a-gazillion snooty New Yorkers crammed into Rafe's ball-room.

ISABEL PARISI TAPPED the delete key until the words *Rafe's ballroom* disappeared from the screen of her laptop. After a moment's thought, she typed in *a glitzy ballroom* instead. Tom might not be able to resist if she dropped such a blatant hint about her plans for New Year's Eve. He could suddenly decide to show up and seek her out.

And that would not do.

Tom Grace, the furniture designer she knew only via e-mail, had been angling for a face-to-face introduction since November, when she'd offhandedly mentioned the enormous potluck Thanksgiving dinner she hosted each year for her unattached friends. He'd practically begged for an invite, in his self-effacing way. Surely she must want to save him from a dull formal dinner at his parents' place in Stamford, where they had the same chestnut stuffing, dry port and stilted conversations every year?

She'd mailed back a silly LOL message as a brush-off, pointing out that some of her guests were refugees from Salvation Army turkey roll, and clearly he hadn't suffered enough to warrant an invitation. He'd accepted the turndown, but had continued to bring up the possibility of their getting together ever since. Often jokingly, sometimes pleadingly, but always in a friendly-joe manner. Except for the occasional suggestion that he wouldn't be averse to becoming romantic.

Oh, horrors.

While Isabel had been able to elude all requests so far,

she dreaded the letter when he issued an ultimatum. She
had no intention of meeting Tom—ever. Although she
liked to call their electronic friendship her "saving
Grace," the truth was that in some ways her e-mails to
Tom had become a confessional. Feeling safely anonymous, she'd been honest with him about herself—fears,
follies and foibles included. As a result, *no one* knew her
the way Tom did, even though they'd never met.

Their correspondence had started almost a year ago,
not long after she'd serendipitously met Arianne and Natalie at the bar at Rafe Monticello's traditional New
Year's Eve gala. The three of them had swiftly become
best friends, but not even Arianne and Natalie knew what
a wake-up jolt Isabel had received that night when she'd
been carrying on merrily as usual, burning her candle at
both ends, thinking she was hurting no one.

Except herself.

You're not worthless, Tom had once written, as only
Tom was allowed, *so why would you treat yourself as if
you are?*

The words had sunk in. Maybe because they'd come
from him, maybe because she'd been ready to hear them.
She'd finally begun to wonder why she wasted so much
of herself on men who had no value to her. Especially
when compared to...well, to Tom.

Isabel shook her head. It was hard to believe she hadn't
scared him away early on. She'd been up-front with him
about her past—and probably future—as a free-spirited
sexual adventuress. He'd taken it in stride, showing none
of the possessive, slavering, bonehead reactions she'd
gotten from other males. But it would've been a different
story if they'd been more than friends. Or if there'd been
even a *possibility* of romance.

She knew from experience. When sex entered the picture, men tend to lose focus on all else.

As she couldn't bear for that to happen with Tom, she kept him at arm's length via computer. Otherwise, it was too easy to predict how, in a few clicks of the keyboard, they'd mutate from jolly good friends to Bootie and the Randy Beast.

And there would go the most intimate relationship she'd ever dared to have.

"Not gonna happen because I won't *let* it happen," she said out loud, then relaxed into a fond smile as she read over the recent e-mail. *Beautilicious?*

He'd been calling her Beauty ever since he'd confessed to buying the September issue of *W* that had published Natalie's short piece about Isabel's textile designs. There'd been a teeny-tiny photo accompanying the article, a shot of a barefoot Isabel in her studio loft, wearing white painter's overalls with her hair all wild. Suitable for the bohemian-artist look the magazine had wanted, but Isabel had thought she'd come across like the Madwoman of Chaillot and had immediately gone out to have her hair whacked off in a short, boyish pixie cut.

Tom had been so flattering in his praise of her beauty and accomplishments that she'd feared he was smitten. To deflect the attention, she'd jokingly responded that then he must be an ugly, terrifying beast with a heart of gold and that was why they got along in such a storybook fashion. What she hadn't said, but implied, was that she was *not* the self-sacrificing fairy-tale heroine type, and so there'd be no chance of wrecking their beautiful friendship.

Isabel tapped the key and returned to her reply to Tom's invitation. Aside from his self-deprecating refrain about being her beast, she had no idea what he looked like. They'd never spoken on the phone, either. Trusting him not to show up one day unannounced was particularly worrisome because she didn't trust easily. After all, they were in the same city, but different boroughs—she in Manhattan and he with a furniture-design studio and factory in Brooklyn. And they did know each other's addresses, having exchanged them for business correspondence early on.

She did, however, believe that Tom would bow to her wishes, even if they should happen to meet. So maybe it was herself she didn't trust when it came to messing up their relationship.

She had male friends she could hang with, and she had lovers of brief duration. The two distinctions were kept entirely separate. It was clear which category Tom had gone into. But if they met and she was physically attracted to him, she probably wouldn't be able to say no. Her willpower was lacking, particularly where men were concerned. They'd wind up sleeping together and then there would be a ninety-nine percent shot that they'd wake up to disaster.

And a one-percent chance of…

"Never mind," Isabel said, glancing at the clock. Natalie would be calling from the cab any moment now, saying she was approaching Elizabeth Street, and Isabel had better be ready.

Buono notte, bello anno! she typed, sticking to the Italian theme in honor of the Monticello's Venetian ball. *Isabel.*

Sure enough, her cell phone began to ring right after she'd mailed the letter. She grabbed a feathered, beribboned mask off the worktable, flung a vintage cashmere cloak over her shoulders and flipped open the phone, holding it to her ear as she raced to the elevator, her dress-up flats thudding on the scarred wood floor.

"I'm on my way, Natalie," she said, glancing back at the loft as she wrenched the heavy industrial elevator doors closed.

Happy New Year's Eve, Tom, my friend.

IN BROOKLYN, still sitting at his desk in the deserted warehouse of Grace Notes even though all his workers had been given the holiday off, Tom read Isabel's latest e-mail with mixed feelings. Despite her spicy outrageousness, the woman exuded warmth and generosity. She never failed to make him smile and feel good about himself...even when she was turning him down.

But he couldn't help wanting more.

Tom knew why the idea scared her. All that Isabel had told him about her background as a teenage runaway and her present habit of flitting from man to man had given him plenty of insight. She claimed to be open and free, but when it came to romantic love she'd shut down long ago.

For months, he'd been puzzling over how to reach her without destroying their friendship. Finally, when she'd mentioned plans to attend a masquerade ball on New Year's Eve, the perfect solution had presented itself.

He would go to her, but not as himself. He would meet her in anonymity. Safety. He would sweep her off her feet before she had time to put up her defenses. If it worked, magnificent. If not, there would still be a chance that he could disappear from her real life and return to his role as the unseen confidant.

Tom lifted a hand to his face. For many reasons, some of them his own, the plan had been immensely appealing from the start.

It had been easy to figure out which party Isabel was attending. Even in New York, center of lavish celebrations and holiday excess, there was only one important Venetian masked ball. Every year, Rafe Monticello, CEO of the family firm, hosted a New Year's Eve party with his mother, the shoe designer, Lucia Monticello. The guest list included celebrities, politicians, socialites and fashion and design professionals. Isabel had been working with the Monticellos for months, designing fabrics for their exclusive use, so naturally she'd be invited.

Tom was not. Grace Notes was doing well, though not well enough to make him more than a nobody among the glitterati. He'd called everyone he knew with contacts to the fashion industry until he'd found a friend of a friend who'd broken a leg at Vail and was willing to barter the coveted invitation for a piece of furniture from Tom's showroom. The secondhand invitation had cost him a satinwood sideboard that retailed for several thousand.

So what, Tom thought, gazing at the garment bag he'd hung on the edge of the door. The mask he'd picked up at a costume shop lay nearby on his drafting table.

He was taking a gamble, but a night with Isabel was worth any risk, any price.

Especially if it led to many more.

2

Near the entrance of the grand ballroom, Isabel tipped her first glass of champagne to her lips. Within moments of her arrival with Natalie Trent and Arianne Sorenson, they'd been greeted by their host, Italian-American playboy Rafe Monticello. Already Natalie was drifting off, absorbed by a masked man she'd spotted in the glittering crowd. She seemed unusually distracted, which was odd when there were so many designer gowns to gape at.

Isabel eyed Arianne, who was stunning in an elegant black dress and matching silk mask that contrasted with her pale hair and skin. Rafe stood beside her, sparring with an amused lift to his lips. The air between them was so electric it crackled.

If Arianne hadn't had such an obvious lech for Rafe, Isabel might have jumped his luscious bod any number of times during the past year. The man was a catch who didn't want to be caught, and that was the best kind as far as she was concerned.

Still, nothing had happened between them, even though they'd met frequently during the course of her work with his mother, Lucia, who was the design genius of Monticello shoes. The spring line of pumps that had used Isabel's richly colored fabrics had been such a success the Monticellos had asked her to license several of her fabrics for their use exclusively. The money and prestige had elevated her career beyond her wildest dreams.

Isabel peered at Rafe from behind her mask. Careerwise, it was fortunate that she'd been conservative—in a manner of speaking—and had gone no further with him than playful flirting.

Even *that* got under Arianne's thin Scandinavian skin. Of course, dear, gentle, uptight Arianne wouldn't admit it…except for making an uncharacteristic snipe about Isabel's penchant for one-night stands.

Little did she know that Tom's wise counseling had led Isabel to make a private resolution to drastically cut back on her more outlandish sexual encounters. She still spoke a big game, true. But her discovery at last year's party that she'd just boinked a man she'd boinked before, and had completely forgotten his face and name in the interim, had been the shock she needed to turn over a new, mature, almost prudish leaf.

Well, maybe not prudish.

She didn't deprive herself. That would be going too far. But she was much choosier about her lovers. Only two of them, the past year.

Which meant that tonight she was allowing herself a treat. Somewhere in this crowd of tuxedoed boy toys there had to be a man who was confident, intelligent and *animale* enough to rouse her libido out of its self-imposed exile.

She wandered deeper onto the dance floor, sipping the remarkable French champagne. Bubbles fizzled on her tongue. Nothing but the best for Rafe's guests. The calculator in Arianne's head must be smoking.

"Mm-mm-mmm." A lantern-jawed hunk looked at Isabel's breasts, bountifully bound by a tight red satin bodice. He grabbed her by the waist and pulled her up against a chest layered with so many muscles she could feel them flexing through his tux. "Hello, sweetcakes," he purred.

"Want to go find one of the private rooms and unmask each other?"

Isabel ran a hand over his chest. It expanded, as did the eager "love muscle" between his thighs. Ugh. She couldn't believe that a one-trick pony like this had ever appealed to her. "Big, strong and hard, that's all I need," she used to say, and sometimes still did for a laugh.

She patted the hunk's bulging pectorals. "Sorry. You're a year too late."

"But it's not midnight yet," he pleaded as she pulled out of his grasp.

"Call me Cinderella—I leave before you come." With a laugh, she swiveled her hips and slid away in a rustle of sheer white chiffon. Beneath the wispy top layer was a miniskirt she'd had made from a length of slightly yellowed but still lovely French Alençon lace. Her only undergarment was a slip of a lace thong. When she moved, her dusky bare skin showed through the shifting fabrics.

She threw a glance over her shoulder. The hunk was watching her departure with his mouth hanging open. A fleck of his spittle caught the light. Blech.

Action, Isabel told herself. She needed a man of action if she wanted to get laid tonight.

She circled the dancing couples, exchanging distant smiles for interested glances. None of the men seemed to possess the extra zing she needed. Blame the near-celibacy of the past year, or Tom's stable influence, but she wanted more than a handsome face and a good body. She wanted a connection.

Granted, a *fleeting* connection.

Maybe she'd lost her taste for the mating game, Isabel mused, stopping to gaze around the immense ballroom. Frescoed dome ceiling, gold-leafed arches, imported Italian stone on the floor—Rafe's mansion was a testimony to wealth and indulgence. The party guests were equally lavish, suited, gowned and masked with no expense spared.

Aside from the strings of twinkling fairy lights overhead, very few lights had been left on. The flickering flames of multiple candelabra and gilt sconces gave the Venetian ball an enchanted Old World feel. The guests were inscrutable in a variety of masks, from elaborate concoctions of feathers and jewels to fantastical creatures and sinister goblins with long, hooked noses.

Excitement stirred in Isabel's blood, despite her doubts. On a night such as this, anything might happen.

A studly waiter slowly moved by in a black-and-white harlequin mask. She looked into his blue eyes as she exchanged her empty champagne flute for a full one, but felt nothing.

Sigh. This could become depressing.

Suddenly an agitated Natalie pushed through the crowd, her high color and red hair stunning with a shimmering gold dress. "He's here," she blurted.

Isabel blinked. "He?"

Natalie drained the flute of champagne gripped in her hand. "Joe." She signaled for the blue-eyed waiter, snagged two flutes from his serving tray and downed the contents of one. "I think he knows it's me, but I ditched him. Oh, God, I don't know how to handle this, Iz. Having my heart trampled again by this guy is not how I want the New Year to start."

"Then don't," Isabel tossed out. If Natalie didn't slow down on the bubbly, she'd be in no shape to handle anything, let alone Joe, the mystery man she'd obsessed over after he'd disappeared from the past New Year's Eve ball. "He can't hurt you if you don't let him."

The band struck up a waltz and they watched the dance

floor for a few moments as the handsome couples swirled by. Isabel itched to join them, but not if it meant being swept into old habits.

Natalie tapped a manicured fingernail against her champagne glass. Still thinking of Joe. "You know…" Behind her gold mask, her eyes gleamed with a wickedness that made Isabel proud. "How do you think he'd feel if I didn't remember him?"

Now they were speaking Isabel's language. She nodded encouragingly. "Good idea. Wound him where it hurts the most—his ego."

"Men and their egos," Natalie said playfully. "Such a fragile thing."

Isabel smiled. "Just be careful. Don't hand him your own heart in the process." Natalie, ever the hopeful romantic, was prone to that.

Satisfied that her friend had been dispatched to enact a suitable payback, Isabel gave in and danced with a couple of eager partners. She turned down their overtures without a second thought. Eventually she found a promising man in a tiger's mask, but as soon as the salsa music started up he began believing he was Antonio Banderas. She was almost glad when Arianne signaled to her from the edge of the dance floor.

The two women met in a corner of the ballroom, where they could speak in relative privacy. Isabel could see that Arianne was upset and immediately she wondered if Rafe was the cause. She hoped so. It was well past time for them to get together. "What's up?"

"I need to do something wild and unpredictable," Arianne announced unexpectedly. She looked down at her plain black dress and frowned.

That was a surprise, Isabel thought. But a pleasant one. After a little prodding, Arianne began babbling about making a resolution to be spontaneous and fun. Her head bobbed up and down, up and down. She looked like Princess Grace on speed.

Isabel advised the blond accountant to go for it, though she did wonder aloud how many champagnes Arianne had downed, not unlike Natalie. Arianne's eyes were bright, almost panicky. Isabel patted her, distracting her with bawdy suggestions like staging screaming orgasms or performing a striptease at the bar. She offered one of the condoms she'd tucked into her cleavage for handy dispersal.

Arianne didn't say so, but even a dunce could have deduced that it was Rafe she wanted to shock. Quite right. If she didn't break out on a night like tonight, it might never happen.

Isabel tried to be helpful. Unfortunately, Arianne ended up excusing herself with a queasy look on her face. ''Never mind. I shouldn't have pulled you away from your latest conquest.''

Isabel had already dismissed the guy from the dance floor. She demurred, surprised to hear herself explaining, ''Tonight I need a man with a little something extra.'' *Like a brain and a true heart,* she thought, then immediately felt as though she had to live up to her bad reputation or Arianne would think she'd become wise and mature.

She spread her hands, measuring the air. ''Ten inches ought to do it.''

Arianne hesitated, and for an instant Isabel thought her friend had guessed she wasn't all that enthused about the available selection. But Arianne only said, with a shrug, ''Happy hunting.''

Uh-huh. Isabel lifted her chin. ''Maybe I'll see you later. At the bar.''

Arianne made a face. "Very funny."

Amused at the thought of cool Arianne doing a down-and-dirty striptease that would make Rafe go volcanic, Isabel wandered around the ballroom, idly glancing over the uninspiring talent. Eventually she found herself in the grand entrance hall, where two of the tuxedo-clad attendants had just finished arranging pyramids of gold shoe boxes. Ah…Rafe's traditional party favor.

Each box bore an inscribed tag. Last year, Isabel had received a slim pair of classic spectator pumps with modest heels. Not her typical footwear, but exactly the shoes she needed to be properly outfitted for her burgeoning career. She'd worn them for business meetings, when she put on one of the serious-career-gal suits that Arianne and Natalie had helped her select.

Perhaps she'd get a pair made with her own fabric this year. Thrilled by the possibility, Isabel ran her fingers over the boxes, looking for her name. Luckily she found it near the top and was able to liberate her gift with only minor reshuffling.

Several couples drifted through the vast hall, on their way to or from the ballroom, paying Isabel no mind. She slipped off to a stylish little Bérgere chair to sit and open her box.

Folding back the layers of red-and-gold tissue paper, she gasped. "But this must be a mistake."

Either Rafe or his staff had screwed up. Isabel pushed her mask up to her forehead to see better. The shoes nestled inside the box were not her style. They were delicate, dressy. The heels were impossibly high. Not at all what she, who lived mostly in sneakers and flat sandals when she wore shoes at all, was accustomed to.

She lifted one of the shoes. A slipper, really, it was so featherlight. Nothing but narrow spike heel, a paper-thin sole and multicolored, crisscrossed ribbons that floated like streamers. Altogether too impractical for the gritty city streets.

But, *mmm*. They were…enticing.

These were shoes that whispered of romance.

Isabel checked the arched doorway to the ballroom. No one was watching. She slipped out of her beaded flats, the same pair she'd worn last year. She wasn't a fashion maven like Natalie, or a savvy bargain hunter like Arianne. Even now that she had a good income, she tended to stick to the flea markets and vintage clothing stores.

It was fabric that was her love. On occasion she found a bolt of a sensuous silk or a velvet so sumptuous she couldn't bear to part with it. She'd bring the material to one of several talented but struggling fashion designers she'd befriended during her own pauper days, to have them create a special item for herself or as a gift for one of her large circle of "family." Rare was the night that she got to wear the sort of dressy gowns that suited these slippers.

Rare, like tonight.

"Well, why not?" she whispered to herself, and bent to slip her bare feet into the new shoes. The red, emerald, gold and purple ribbons had been made to cross her instep, wind around her ankle and up her calf. Weaving them in and out made her legs look like matching maypoles.

She set her feet and rose, wobbling when she reached full height, almost as if she'd mounted a pair of stilts. She took a few steps, knock-kneed, hands out for balance. Natalie would laugh to see her.

By the refracted light of the crystal chandelier, Isabel caught a glimpse of herself in a tall Venetian mirror hung among an impressive display of Italian old-master oil paintings. Her chin lifted, her neck elongated. She touched her palm to her strapless bodice, swished her lace and chiffon skirt back and forth with the other hand. ''Goodness,'' she murmured.

The steep shoes made her seem quite swanlike. Almost regal.

Certainly very different from the runaway ragamuffin she'd once been—and still thought herself to be, deep inside.

Suddenly the double front doors were swept open and a wintry wind swirled through the hall. A butler appeared from nearby, requesting the latecomer's proof of invitation. The Monticellos' exclusive, engraved invitation was proffered.

There was a minor fuss as the new arrival's shoulders were swept free of snow and his topcoat carried away by the cloakroom attendant. The doors had been quickly swung shut, but the cold was in Isabel's lungs. Freezing her immobile.

The man who stood before her seemed to have come straight from a surreal dream. He was tall, lean and elegant in his tuxedo. All that she could see of his face was the lower half—a wide, strong jaw, a dimpled chin and an incredibly sensual mouth. Above that, he wore a magnificent lion's head mask, intricately carved and worked in a crackled Renaissance gold leaf, the flaring mane depicted in extravagant swirls.

Though Isabel took all of him in, she was riveted by his eyes. She had no idea what color they were. Who could bother with color when the depths were this hot, this reaching, and molten with an immediate desire?

He stared until her throat had closed so tight she couldn't breathe. Warmth had surged into her cheeks, a sharp contrast to the numbing cold elsewhere. Feeling exposed, she carefully lowered her mask, not surprised to see that her raised hand was trembling.

The stranger in the lion's mask approached.

The music from the ballroom swelled to a crescendo. She was lifted, weightless, exalted by the clear-cut rightness of this meeting.

Oh, yes. She'd found her man for the night.

He offered his elbow. "Shall we?"

She was almost afraid to touch him. Very unlike her.

"Yes, why not?" she made herself say, throwing her head back and laughing throatily as she took his arm.

At the same moment, she turned, forgetting the shoes she'd just put on. Unaccustomed to the heels, she lost her balance and might have fallen if her escort hadn't gripped her arms, holding her up. He put one arm around her waist, taking her weight as she sprawled against his chest.

Embarrassment scorched her face. She laughed again, straightening with a snap. "I'm not usually so clumsy. It's these heels."

Her companion glanced down. "They're dangerous weapons." His gaze lingered. "You could put an eye out."

"Only of those who are so rude enough to stare."

His head came up. The lights glinted off the golden mask. His eyes were shadowed, mysterious. "I'll risk it," he said. "You are such a beauty it's impossible for me to take my eyes off you."

Tom, Isabel thought.

But it couldn't be.

3

"Do I KNOW YOU?" Isabel asked. She and the stranger stood at the entrance to the ballroom. Her hand was on his arm and his palm covered her fingers—warm, encompassing, exhilarating. He had such a potent *zing* she was snap-crackle-popping with it.

"We've never met." His voice was as soft and rich as a bolt of the finest imported velvet. "I'm certain that I would remember you."

"But we're in masks," she pointed out. She was trying to think how to handle their encounter. He couldn't be Tom. Tom didn't know where she was. He might have guessed where she was—it wouldn't take a rocket scientist to figure out her destination since she had a public connection to the Monticellos. Still...no. She'd been clear with him. They weren't to meet. Tom was home eating pastrami on rye and watching the ball drop on TV. The man standing beside her was a total stranger.

Nevertheless, she should tread carefully.

"I did see your face," he said. "When I first came in, before you lowered your mask."

"Then you have me at a disadvantage."

"Shall we exchange names?"

"No!" She winced at her vehemence. It had come out of instinct, but why was she so alarmed?

For caution's sake, she thought. That's all.

"We're supposed to remain masked until midnight,"

she explained, tilting her head to look at him. His hair was a tawny blond, thick and wavy, longer than her own.

The barrier of the mask was both titillating and frustrating. She wanted to look at his face. On the other hand, keeping their disguises in place would suit her intentions. If he made love the way she hoped, she would need that protection.

And then, there was something so decadent and forbidden about sex with a masked stranger....

She shivered.

"Care to dance?" he asked.

She nodded wordlessly and the stranger swept her onto the dance floor. The orchestra had been switching between beats all evening. She could swing, she could samba, she could even fake a flamenco, but she'd never waltzed before. Surprisingly, the graceful motion of the classic dance came easily to her, thanks to her partner's strong, guiding arms. Even the steep heels weren't too much of a hindrance, not when she was dancing on air.

"We have less than thirty minutes until midnight," he said.

Was that all? Her high spirits swooped in sync with the dance.

Only a half hour, she thought. *Thirty minutes to live out a fantasy with the man of a lifetime.*

He angled his head toward her ear. "Any ideas on what we should do with the time?"

For once, she was too intimidated to be blunt about wanting him naked and sweaty and pounding deep inside her. There was more going on between them than her initial plan for a fast, anonymous sexual fling to ring in the New Year.

She turned her face away from his, just slightly. "We should play it by ear."

"You have lovely ears," he whispered. His tongue flickered near her lobe; he breathed against her neck. Her skin became covered in goose bumps. "And an intoxicating scent."

She didn't wear perfume—all natural, that was her.

Isabel shifted nervously in his arms as he drew her closer. Together, they were magnetic. She wanted to close her eyes, lose herself...

"Your hair is so short."

Her eyes flashed open. "So?"

He slid a hand over her bare shoulder, his fingers tickling her nape. "It shows your neck." He made a sound in his throat. "Makes me want to kiss it."

She relaxed and leaned her head on his shoulder carefully so that she didn't crush the white plumes that crowned her mask. "Hold that thought."

"Ah, but you've filled my head with wicked thoughts. Some of them have to spill out into words."

That was intriguing. So few men knew how to seduce a woman with their brain as well as their body. "Mmhmm?" she hummed, encouraging him.

The music had shifted into a string melody that was pure romance. They moved even closer to each other, one pair of hands remaining clasped while his free hand roamed at will, not in a presumptuous or sleazy way, but with just the right touch as he caressed her shoulder blades, stroked her spine, then finally settled his splayed fingers on her hip.

He touched his cheek to her head. "Your feathers are ticklish."

She imagined plucking one and running it down his naked body, knowing that all she had to do was signal assent and they would be doing exactly so. The palm of her free hand itched where it rested on his chest. If she moved it slightly, she could slide a fingertip past the studs of his shirt…

Ahh. His skin was hot satin.

He gave no sign he'd noticed her small caress. She uncurled her finger and stroked it inside his shirt again, bolder this time, savoring the electric sensation that even such an insignificant contact engendered. What would it be like to slither against his entire length, skin to skin?

She had to know.

"Can we find a more private location for this?" he asked.

Isabel lifted her chin, lips parting. "I'd like—" *Nothing better.*

But something made her stop and swallow the rest of her sentence rather than admit her instant lust out loud. The attraction between them was so amazing, so pure and strong, she had to remind herself that he was a total stranger. Even at her wildest moments, she'd chosen her partners with some caution, always keeping in mind a lesson learned the hard way: that the worst of men could be cruel and abusive. And that women, no matter how careful, were physically vulnerable.

She needed a safety net.

Rafe, she thought. He was the kind of honorable, loyal man she could rely on.

"Don't be in such a hurry," she chided her dance partner. "You haven't even spoken to our host yet. You do know Rafe Monticello, yes?"

The stranger smiled at her, his heavy eyelids lowering as he gazed into her face. "You want to check me out with him?"

She flipped her partner a sassy grin. "Sure. My judgment can't be trusted once I'm champagne-impaired. Rafe vets all of my New Year's Eve flings."

His smile dropped away. "*All* of them?"

She concealed her sudden disappointment. Of course he would pounce on that. The old double standard rears its macho head.

"Never mind," he said abruptly.

So that's it, she thought as the mystery man stepped away—but he didn't let go. Keeping her hand, he led her across the dance floor, through the guests clustered in small groups around the edges of the room.

"None of your previous flings matter now that I've found you." He scanned the crowd with a visible impatience that was very flattering. Her excitement took hold again. "I don't see Monticello. Do you?"

She dragged her gaze off the stranger. "He was dancing, earlier, with my—" She stopped just before identifying Arianne as her close friend. It was best if she left no clues. After this night was over, it would be *over*.

Her dance partner cocked his head, radiating curiosity. "You're not Monticello's sister, are you?"

She shook her head.

"His wife? I would have to draw the line there."

"Rafe is a notoriously single playboy," she said. How could any guest not know that?

"Just checking," he said. "I wouldn't want to insult the host by stealing his, hmm…girlfriend?"

"Trust me. I have no personal connection to Rafe." She thought of Arianne. "At least not the kind that would lead him to fight for my virtue."

The masked man dropped the teasing smile and put his arms around her to say in thrillingly formal tones, "I don't intend to dishonor you. Given the chance, I hope to worship every inch of your precious body with a most reverent and attentive care." He added a suggestive chuckle. "Albeit, in very inventive and naughty ways."

Isabel's breath caught in her chest. He was handing her no line. She believed him, from the wavering fronds of her feathers to the tips of her tingling toes.

Without a doubt, he was the *one*.

She let out the breath. Her voice must have lifted on the same gust of air because her usual husky tones tinkled like the chimes of a Christmas chorus. "If that's truly the case, you must follow me upstairs."

"HOW WELL DO YOU KNOW this place?" Tom said, after they'd stolen up the curved staircase with their hands linked as if they were naughty children who'd been on a midnight spy mission. Isabel had liberated a bottle of champagne from one of the monogrammed ice buckets that were set up on gilt-legged tables at various points around the room.

"Well enough. This is my second invitation to Rafe's New Year's Eve ball."

"My first," he said, lying without compunction. He was in this now, all the way. It was happening so fast, and felt so right there was no time for doubt.

Isabel stopped midway along the second-story gallery that encircled the ballroom. "I knew you couldn't have been here last year. I'd have found you."

"How?"

"Intuition." She pressed against him, moving her entire body in a seductive caress. "Pheromones."

He smoothed her feathers. "Careful, or you'll have me believing in fate."

"For tonight, we both do." She tugged his hand. "Come on, I know just the place."

As the party carried on below, they hurried along the carpeted gallery, passing dimly lit hallway openings and niches carved into the stucco walls, filled with museum-quality pieces of artwork—marble statues, glazed urns, small oil paintings murky with crackled varnish. The luxury was little more than a blur to Tom. He'd almost decided not to come at all, until a sudden spurt of anger with his timidity had gotten him moving.

This could be his lone chance to be with Isabel. He *had* to try.

"Here," she said, stopping before an alcove.

"Here?" Tom asked. The corners of his mouth lifted.

The alcove was not completely private, but it was quite a setting for seduction. Burgundy velvet curtains swagged the archway of a nook that was only big enough for a small round table and a deep recamier with thickly rolled arms and walnut legs carved into winged lions. It was piled with pillows and lushly padded, upholstered in a tufted burgundy velvet. The walls were a striped raw silk. The enclosure was lit by a pair of gilt sconces dripping with amber cut-crystal bobeches.

Isabel set the bottle of champagne on the side table. "Big enough for two."

Tom's grin expanded. Was this really going to happen so easily? "Sure, if we're willing to share our space."

"Aren't we?" She turned and took hold of his black satin lapels to pull him down with her as she sank onto the chaise. He landed on all fours, holding himself above her as he found her mouth. Slowly lowering his body onto hers, he deepened the kiss degree by degree until they were caught up in flames. Their tongues brushed, twisted, plunged, lost to the total abandon of the moment.

Except that the moment stretched into minutes, and then into five, and still they hadn't stopped kissing. Their masks ground against each other, shedding tiny red feathers and flakes of gold leaf. A rhinestone popped off Isabel's mask and pinged against the glass bottle of cham-

pagne. She only laughed, her neck arching as he pressed
a hand to her forehead, tilting her face so he could drink
kiss after wet kiss from her open mouth. His hunger was
overwhelming. It was wild and huge and it went far beyond even his most intimate fantasies of how he would
be with Isabel.

"Please let me lift your mask," he said. "I have to
kiss your eyes, your nose, your forehead...."

A couple walked by arm in arm, laughing indulgently
when they spied the lovers in the alcove.

"Pull the drapes," Isabel said hurriedly, "and I promise you'll get to see all of me."

He fumbled with the gold tasseled cords, freeing them.
The drapes dropped shut, enclosing them in dim privacy.
While the heavy fabric muted the sounds of the party,
they could still hear the excitement as the midnight zenith
approached.

Isabel reached out a hand to hold the curtain back, and
they both peered through the crack to the fairy lights
strung from the railing to the central chandelier. Tom was
surprised to realize how erotic and stimulating it was to
know that they would soon be in the throes of lovemaking while some twenty-odd feet away, the crowd carried
on unaware.

He studied Isabel for a moment before dropping his
head to trail kisses along her bare arm. "The mask," he
said.

"But we can't know each other."

He stopped, kneeling above her. "Why?" If the evening was a success, he fully intended to reveal his identity. She would be shocked, of course. But he'd make her
see that this was the only way. She'd come to understand.

Isabel hesitated. "Be-because this is a fantasy."

Tom's voice dropped, grating in his throat. "Only a fantasy?"

"Only...?" She shook her head, smiling as she regained control. "No. That implies less. What I want from you tonight is more than either of us has ever dared dream."

4

"FOR THAT, I need to see your face."

"Why?" Isabel asked.

"Call it *my* fantasy." The stranger stroked a hand over her upraised thigh, sliding the layers of her dress higher.

She shivered with the hot-and-cold sensations of wanting him so badly that she feared what it meant. He was asking her to reveal herself. Not an unreasonable request, except she couldn't help feeling that all her emotions might spill out with the lifting of her mask.

Pfft. Nonsense. She was made of sterner stuff.

"On one condition," she said. "You have to promise you won't try to find me afterward."

There was a long silence, and she thought she'd lost him. The deep squeezing pain she suddenly felt surprised her. Because...because...he seemed to promise so much more than an affair with a stranger. Yet that was supposed to be all she wanted from him.

At last he nodded. "I promise not to look for you."

Her stomach swirled with unusual trepidation as he leaned forward, reaching for her mask. He'd already seen her face, after all. She was risking very little.

He slid his fingertips beneath the feathers to find the hard edge of the mask, then pulled it past her brow, stretching the elastic until it snapped off the back of her head. The trailing ends of the scarlet ribbon trim slipped across her cheeks as he lifted the mask away. The air was cool on her heated skin.

His dark eyes stared at her from behind the lion's face. "You're very beautiful."

Isabel had grown up believing she was ugly. Her stepfather had called her a Heinz 57 mutt because of her mixed heritage—her mother was Indian and Asian, and her late father was Italian with a mélange of other European countries thrown in for good measure. She'd also been gawky and skinny and too poor to dress nicely. Only when she'd come into her own as a young woman away from that hated house and developed a circle of loving friends of every ethnicity had she accepted herself for being uniquely American.

"Cat's eyes," he said, tracing a finger over the tilt of her lids.

She flicked her tongue. "Make me purr."

"My pleasure." He touched his mask. "Should I take this off first?"

"Leave it," she said instantly. It wasn't that she didn't want to see his face. In fact, she was ridden with an intense curiosity. But the secrecy was even better—and safer. "Leave your tuxedo on, too."

He cocked his head. His eyes glinted.

"It's part of the fantasy," she said, not knowing how to put into words the image she had in her head of her supine naked body spread before a fully clothed male, a wild, beastly stranger who would take her with savage lust boiling in his veins....

Oh, who was she kidding with her resolution for restraint? Give her a shot with the right man and she was as wicked as ever!

"Whatever you want," he said.

She lay back on the pillows, her arms reaching overhead in a luxurious stretch. Her legs were immodestly parted, tangled around his waist, one foot dangling near the floor. "I want you to open the champagne. It will be the new year soon, and we must have some at midnight."

He leaned across her to snag the bottle. She sank her fingers into his thick hair, using it to draw him to her for another kiss. She nibbled at his jaw, licked the small cleft in his chin, suckled on his lower lip, all the while resisting the urge to get his name. "I'm going to call you Leo," she announced.

He had rested the cold bottle against her abdomen. "I'll call you…Puss."

She laughed, giving another lazy stretch. *"Rowrrr."*

"Or maybe *Bella* would be more appropriate."

She jerked up to her elbows. *"Bella?"*

"Because this evening has an Italian theme." He bowed his head. "And, of course, in honor of your remarkable beauty."

"Hmm." She waited for the prickles of suspicion to pass. "True beauty takes longer to know. I prefer Puss."

A silence fell between them, relieved only by the sounds of celebration from the ballroom. "Leo" had peeled the foil from the champagne and was working the cork free, but the task didn't require that much concentration. Had she put him off by pointing out that he didn't know the inner her—and never would?

"Puss it is," he said. "You do realize that we have no glasses?"

"We'll have to share the bottle."

His hot gaze skimmed her body. "Or lap it up from elsewhere."

With a loud *pop,* the cork flew from the bottle, bouncing off the velvet drape. The champagne foamed up, spattering both of them before he brought it to his mouth and took a long swallow.

"Now I'm wet," she said, laughing as she brushed at the spots dampening her satin top.

He grinned and passed her the bottle. "Now?"

She took a swig before reclining again. Indeed, a liquid heat had been pooling between her thighs from the moment they'd met. "You know what I mean."

He glanced over her, trying to frown. "I'll have to remove your dress."

She winked. "Watch the claws."

"Yours or mine?"

Her laughter bubbled. "Also the whiskers and teeth."

His lips pulled back and he clicked his very white teeth. "Don't worry. I've never injured anyone."

"Well, mmm, then I surrender myself to you." She set the bottle aside and reached for her skirts, gathering them up in her hands, pulling them toward her waist as she twisted against the cushions. She was on fire, unable to keep still. "I think I'm in heat."

"I feel that." His palm coasted along her thighs as he pushed her skirts to her waist. With a low growl, he pressed his face among the chiffon, against her belly. He inhaled. "I smell that."

Desire exploded in Isabel. She wanted to rip the dress off. Instead she took his head in her hands, moaning at the swipe of his tongue as he found her hot skin beneath the layers of chiffon and lace. He laved her, the mask riding up as he rubbed his face over her stomach and thighs before going to the center of her need, nipping at the lace thong, his tongue darting beneath it to lap at the moist heat flowing from her.

She looked down. *Oh my.* His head had completely disappeared beneath the poufy dress.

Her thighs opened wider. "Please…"

He came up for air, his mask askew. She caught a split-second glimpse of a sizable nose and warm brown eyes before he readjusted it. Before she could comment, he had snapped her thong with one sharp tug and tossed the flimsy piece of lace to the floor, looking only at her face. Almost glaring.

A tiny fear tickled her nerve endings, making her give a start and a shiver. The sense of danger was sweet. Delicious.

Leo said nothing. No need. She could read his thoughts as he leaned over her. He wanted her naked. *Now.*

She gave no thought to the dress as he dragged the red satin from her breasts, snaps popping, the zipper at the back giving a metallic screech as it tore apart. The condoms she'd tucked inside her bodice scattered. Together, they shoved the dress away, and she was nude but for the high-heeled sandals. He glanced once at the complicated ribbons, then reached for the champagne.

She crossed her arms over her abdomen, almost wanting to cover up from his eyes. "Uh-uh," he said, gently pulling her arms free so he had an unobstructed view of her body. His gaze traced over her skin as hot as a sparkler, shooting off snippets of fire. She was burning up.

As if he knew how she felt, he rolled the cold bottle over her thighs, for one erotic moment nudging it against her inflamed sex—the tingling shock fantastic against her clit—before he pressed the cool glass to her tummy, her ribs, and finally tilted the weighty vessel to its side and slid the neck between her breasts. Icy champagne spewed into her cleavage, bubbles fizzling, wet and ticklish. She let out a little *yip,* but immediately his mouth was there, sucking the sparkling wine from her skin.

She breathed a sibilant sigh. "Oh, yesss."

He moved the bottle, deliberately tipping more of the champagne over her breasts. Following the path of liquid with his tongue and mouth, he alternately licked and tasted, squeezing a luxurious handful of her left breast while he butterfly-flicked her right nipple with his teeth. She arched into the caress, her legs twined around his hips.

Suddenly high-pitched laughter and several babbling female voices came from the other side of the curtain. Isabel flinched, then pantomimed relief as the party guests moved on in the direction of the staircase. "Hurry, it's almost midnight," one of them said.

Leo looked at Isabel. "Almost midnight. Do you want to come before it?"

"On the dot of," she glibly challenged. "There's no better way to start off a new year. Do you think you can manage that?"

He checked his watch, then looked at her breasts. "I can try."

"Try lower."

"Here?" He edged backward, spilling champagne into the hollow of her navel. Her stomach muscles twitched. He put his mouth against her skin and drank. Then re-filled and drank more.

"Lower," she said.

"Ahhh." He pulled upright and grabbed a pillow, sliding it beneath her so her bottom was raised. His hands stroked over the entire length of her legs, pulling them free from around him before lifting her by the back of her knees, spreading her open, setting her spike heels at either edge of the width of the chaise. Then he retrieved the bottle and took a lusty swig while he gazed at the ripe, ready display.

She swallowed nervously. The waiting was sheer torture. Her inner muscles clenched and released, clenched and released.

His eyes found hers. He raised the bottle. "Want some?"

She nodded. He slanted over her, the lapels of his tux catching on her taut nipples. She threw back her head and opened her mouth, and he poured champagne into it until she was sputtering and laughing, trying to swallow as he kissed her.

"You taste better than champagne," he whispered, dragging his tongue down her body until he was back where he started.

Before she could say anything, the mouth of the bottle touched between her legs. She tensed. "Tell me if you want to stop," he said, but she shook her head, looking at the dull golden gleam of the lion's mask positioned right there between her thighs. She wanted the champagne in her and his tongue in her and...

His fingers opened her, stroke by stroke. She began to move her hips, begging for it. Then finally the smooth glass lip was eased slightly inside her body and she saw the green bottle tilt upward and felt with a head-spinning rush the effervescence as cold champagne spilled against her hot flesh. Instantly his mouth replaced the bottle. Slick glass gave way to warm velvet as his tongue licked inside her, slurping up the champagne.

She pressed the heels of her palms against her eyes, riveted by the sensation. "Again."

And once more he put the bottle to her, using her as a cup. First came the cold spill of champagne, then the warm soft blade of his tongue.

A deep tremor ran through her. "Again."

Downstairs, the noise level increased as the countdown to midnight began. "Ten, nine..."

The bottle touched her intimately, dipping at an angle.

"Eight, seven…"

There was a moment of exquisite pressure and then the fizzy champagne.

"Six, five…"

She tightened her muscles on the foaming liquid as her lover's mouth replaced the bottle. His tongue thrust deeper than before, sucking out the champagne, probing, then withdrawing.

"Four, three…"

The pleasure gathered force inside her. She cried out as he filled her with his fingers and then his tongue again, hardened like an arrow-tip as it flicked over the tight pearl of her clit. Her hips rose to meet the rush of sensation, every tendon in her legs strung taut.

"Two, one…"

The tension and pleasure and pain exploded inside her. She shattered, coming in hard waves against his mouth as she added her keening voice to the clamor of noisemakers going off and crashing cymbals and people cheering in an elated chorus.

"Happy New Year!"

"DON'T STOP NOW," she said a few moments later, when the world had quit spinning.

"Mmm." She felt the vibration of his voice against her tummy. "Giving you a breather, Puss."

"I don't need one," she said, even though she was panting. Her lungs hurt as if she'd run a race, but she took a deep breath to ease them, eager to continue. Her hand brushed through his hair. In the ballroom, the revelry went on.

She rocked her hips to be sure she had his attention. "I forgot to tell you."

His head lifted. "What?"

"How I prefer my orgasms."

"Oh?"

"Like doughnuts," she said, tugging at his shoulders. She sat up, reaching around his waist to pull off his cummerbund. She began working on the studs of his shirt. Skin—she needed to feel his skin.

"Hot from the deep fryer?" he guessed as she gave up on the studs and pulled the tail of his shirt from his pants. "One right after the other?"

"Nope." *Ahh.* Her hands touched bare chest. She ran her fingers over the tight muscled terrain, slick with a light mist of perspiration. She smiled. How had he managed to hold off?

He moaned when her fingers dipped toward his zipper. "Wait. I have to know. How do you prefer your orgasms and your doughnuts?"

She rubbed her belly against his arousal. "Filled."

After a moment of silence, he laughed with delight. "Yeah. They're better for me that way, too."

"Well, then?" She tilted her head toward his.

They kissed. She had both hands on him, toying with him, until he let out a soft "Argh," and pushed her onto her back, opening her thighs as he knelt between them and released his erection. It was long and thick and impossibly hard, and her tongue curled just looking at it.

"I'll do it," she said, sitting up and finding one of the condoms that had fallen to the floor. She took her time sheathing him, wanting to feel the pulsing of his flesh in her hands. He knelt obediently before her, until she ducked to lick the dewdrop off the head of his penis, and then he pushed forward into her waiting mouth with a guttural sigh. She gave one long, savoring suck before fitting the condom to him and rolling it down his slickened shaft.

"Come here." He put his hands under her bottom and lifted, centering her against his erection.

Molten with need, she let go, her head and shoulders falling back on the pillows, her spine bowed into an inverted *C*. She pressed her palms over her breasts, covering the aching, erect tips. When she opened her eyes, the alcove seemed to have turned upside down. "You come here." She tweaked her nipples. "I need your mouth."

"You need *this*," he said, and speared into her with a thrust of his hips.

"Oh!" He'd filled her so completely the air was driven from her lungs. She gasped once, twice, and then he was there, kissing her as they rocked back and forth like a boat lapped by waves. Dipping low, then rising, dipping, rising, his mouth drawing on her nipple so the desire flowed through them in a continuous loop.

A new strength seeped into her, and she was able to bring her legs up, hooking them over his bobbing rear end. He caught the back of one knee and she kicked her foot into the air, the colored ribbons of her new stilettos catching the golden light from the sconces.

"Yes, yes, yes," she heard herself saying when the tempo quickened.

The lion's mask appeared in front of her face. He was braced on his arms now, riding her relentlessly into the climax brewing between them like an electric storm over the ocean. She grabbed his lapels and stared into his eyes, memorizing them.

This was it. Almost over.

She stopped thinking then, surrendering to the flashes of intense pleasure that blitzed her spasming body. The stranger who'd become her lover was above her, thrusting, plunging. Even when she closed her eyes she heard him panting, and soon grunting animal noises as he went rigid and pulsed inside her, over and over with such intensity she knew the only way it could have been better was if there'd been no barriers between them, no condom, no mask—

What the—?

She'd lost her mind! She didn't want babies any more than she wanted a husband. Or even a name. One fabulous fling didn't change that.

She shoved hard at his shoulders, and he backed away instantly, sliding out of her. She drew up her legs and slammed her eyes shut, waiting for the pleasure—and emotion—to diminish. Dammit. What was she going to *do?*

No way could she let a stranger see that he'd somehow managed to reach a place inside her that was forbidden.

"What's wrong?"

She peered through her lashes. Leo had straightened his mask and was now discarding the condom and putting himself back together, as if this had been an ordinary event. And maybe it was, for him, as it had once been for her. Well, she could pretend it still was, right?

"Nothing." She sat up, legs coiled, arms crossed over her breasts. "I just realized how exposed—um, how embarrassing it would be if someone had peeked in on us. I hope nobody heard."

He cocked his head at the sounds of music and laughter. "Don't worry. No one's paying attention."

"Could you hand me my dress?"

The bouffant skirt rustled as he picked the gown off the floor. "Sorry. It's ripped."

"S'okay." She slid it over her head, in an unusual

hurry to cover up. The zipper gaped, torn at the seam. She'd have to clamp her arms to her sides to hold up the bodice.

"Take my jacket." He shrugged out of it.

"But—" She bit her lip, not sure how to explain her reluctance. Either he'd misunderstood her conditions, or he was hoping she'd changed her mind about exchanging names, making contact. This was the first time she'd even considered it, even if only for a second or two.

"Don't worry about returning it."

Okay, that took care of that! She slipped into the jacket and pulled it close around her breasts. The torn thong lay on the floor near the velvet drape. She snatched up the piece of lace and hurriedly shoved it into a pocket. "Well…"

"So this is it?"

"I guess so."

"Rather abrupt."

"I move fast."

He chuckled, deepening the grooves around his mouth. "No kidding."

Good, she thought. *He was taking their parting well. Great, in fact. Just great.*

"Hell of a New Year's Eve party," he said.

She stood, not surprised to find that her knees were weak and her ankles wobbly. She gripped the jacket tighter. "Yes, Rafe always throws quite the bash."

The lion's eyes flashed. He gestured with his dimpled chin. "I wasn't talking about the party out there."

"Um."

"Is there any chance—"

"No," she snapped. "You made a promise."

"So I did," he said in a soft voice. She sensed there

was more to the simple words than she was prepared to know.

"I have to go."

He settled back on the chaise among the disarranged pillows, folding his arms behind his head. His shirt was still half undone, hanging out of his pants. "Fine."

The wish to lift his mask and see his face was so strong she had to make fists and shove them into the pockets of his jacket. Her nails gouged into her palms. "Fine."

She didn't move.

His mouth twitched. "Happy New Year, Isabel."

Shock bolted through her. *"How do you know my name?"*

Several tense moments passed.

Finally he spoke. "It was on the shoe box, downstairs where we met."

She trembled all over, wanting to stamp her foot, to scream, to grab him and kiss him until this strange mixture of desire and fascination and fear was gone.

"Forget you know it," she said, and threw open the drapes and ran away.

5

Tommy-boy, I feel like that old Elton John song, I think it was Elton, the one that went "someone changed, someone changed, someone changed my life tonight" or lyrics in that vein. I don't remember and I don't even know what I'm saying. I mean typing. Letters r swimming on the screen. As predicted, too much of that damn Dom…and oh Tommy it was on me and in me oh-oh-oh was it IN me. You don't know.

I don't know. What to feel what to do….

Why'm I writing? You should delete this. Should I delete this? Sleep now brunch tomorrow.

OH GOD BRUNCH!!!

Iz

TOM PACED the living room of his apartment in Brooklyn, a coffee mug in hand. Seven in the morning and he'd already had three cups. He'd arrived home from the Monticello ball early enough, considering, but he'd barely slept. Around five, he'd been up working on a design for the Harricks' custom sofa. In preliminary sketches the lines were simple, almost Japanese. But this morning it had come out looking a lot like an Italian Renaissance recamier. He'd balled up the drawings, sunk a three-pointer in the trash can and gone to check his e-mail.

He hadn't expected to hear from Isabel so soon, but apparently she'd written to him right after the party, half-way drunk or maybe high on their mutually astonishing experience.

A couple of hours and three cups of coffee later, he'd finished analyzing her note and concluded that the good news outweighed the bad.

Bad: Isabel seemed to have no idea it had been him.

Good: Even though she had the lyric wrong, she knew that her life was changed.

Semicoherently.

It was a start. On the other hand, in a couple of hours she'd be having brunch with Natalie and Arianne. He knew damn well the three of them would pick apart every nuance of the evening—being typical women—and Isabel's opinion might swing in another direction, particularly if they figured out his identity.

His idiot secret identity. What a bad idea that had been, even if he'd only kept the mask on at Isabel's insistence. And, admittedly, out of some reluctance of his own.

He'd promised Isabel he wouldn't look for her, knowing he was tricking her with semantics. Because he didn't have to look. He already knew exactly where to find her.

He stopped pacing and stared out the big arched windows overlooking Washington Street and a glimmer of the East River. The top benefit of living in Brooklyn was having a lot of space for half the money a similar apartment in Manhattan would have cost. He'd been able to afford both a two-bedroom apartment with suitable studio space and the large factory with an office and reception area nearby, which housed Grace Notes. The business was a small concern, for now. Fifteen employees built his designs and shipped them to trendy design stores, mainly in the New York area.

He wasn't even close to being a millionaire like Rafe Monticello. Tom had always wondered if Isabel had an interest in the playboy, considering how often and with such relish she'd written about their dealings. But not anymore. All he had to do was remember the fierce, erotic way she'd made love to *him* last night. That had said it all.

Unless she was that way with all her partners.

Unless, when the mask came off, she'd feel differently.

The caffeine gnawed at Tom's empty stomach. Bad train of thought, that was. In spite of his less-than-active love life, he was experienced enough to know that their connection, which had encompassed more than a phenomenal physical attraction, didn't happen very frequently. Never, for him.

And the chances were that he had been as special for Isabel as she had been for him. No question, he *had* to follow through on his plan to reveal himself.

As for Monticello...

For a few disastrous seconds the previous night, Tom had been sure Isabel was going to lead him to their host. Not only would Rafe have failed to recognize him as an invited guest, the man probably would've had Tom thrown out on his ear when they discovered the gilded invitation supplied to the henchmen at the door had been meant for someone else. Fortunately, Isabel had been easily distracted.

The sun was coming up all gold and pink over the iron scaffolding of the Brooklyn Bridge, but the beauty was wasted on him this morning. He was wondering if he should come clean *now,* before Isabel and her friends concluded that he'd taken advantage of his inside knowledge for an evening of unconditional hot sex.

Yeah, guilty as charged. Except that he was thinking conditional all the way.

Isabel would be pissed at that, too.

Tom refilled his coffee mug. He grabbed the laptop off his desk, stretching the cable to the couch by the windows. His Burmese cat, Polly, was stretched out along the back cushion, her sable fur lit by the morning sun.

His mind went to Isabel, stretched out among the pillows, lithe curves, tawny skin, her deep brown cat's eyes blinking with lazy pleasure. He'd never known a woman as confident in her skin as Isabel. As sexual.

Her breasts were sumptuous, her nipples the color of café au lait. The sleek, boyish haircut had surprised him, even though she'd mentioned it in a previous e-mail. But her hair—matched by the triangle of dark curls below—really was the dark mahogany he'd imagined when she'd first described her mixed ethnicity. He would have been satisfied if all that he had done was stare at her for the entire night. Not merely for her physical beauty, but because of the astonishing fact that there she'd been—his spirited, brazen, tender Isabel, in person at last after so many shared confidences.

Ah, but holding her, kissing her, loving her…that had been almost beyond belief. A staggering development.

When he'd first made the decision to crash Monticello's New Year's Eve party, he'd realized that the end result might be the last of his e-mail friendship with Isabel. It could be that he'd traded one night with the real woman for a thousand touching letters.

It would be worth it, he'd told himself. Now, in the light of day, he wasn't so sure. He knew Isabel's vulnerability, her reluctance to face intimacy. Perhaps he should have remained satisfied with what she was comfortable giving.

She'd been unnerved last night, when the sex was over and she'd realized that the closeness wouldn't end as easily. She'd started to withdraw even before he'd purposely said her name. By the time her friends arrived for brunch, she'd be in full panic mode. Intimacy was her anathema—she'd admitted that herself in several of her most heartfelt late-night-and-I'm-alone-and-lonely e-mails. This morning, she'd be so scared she'd find a way to toast him crisper than a bagel.

"Worth the risk, Polly," Tom said to the cat, who only yawned.

He logged on to his e-mail server, hoping like hell the right words would come to him. Because he had to tell Isabel that he loved her, even if that scared her away forever.

Before reopening her post-masquerade note, he clicked on the file he'd made of her previous e-mails. Their first contact had come when he'd written to request samples of her fabrics in hopes of finding a new source for his next line of home furnishings. After only a few innocuous business letters, a personal touch had crept in. He'd mentioned having tickets to the Knicks. She said the name *Cholly Knickerbocker* always made her giggle. Soon they were chatting back and forth a couple of times a week. Then every day. Every night. He'd begun saving her notes. And one morning he'd awakened thinking about how to describe his dream to Isabel—his dream, for chrissake—and then he'd known that he'd fallen in love, not only with a woman he'd never met, but with one who refused to even consider the possibility of giving a relationship between them a try.

Tom read snippets of Isabel's notes at random.

...I left home when I was sixteen, but I wasn't a run-away. Ripe for trouble, huge chip on my shoulder, and scared absolutely shitless the entire time, but still, I knew that I had to run toward a better way of living. In those early days I was too beaten down to have a clear idea of what that was, but...

...Tom Grace! Honest to God, how can I possibly respect a man who doesn't agree that Julie Taymor is a genius?!! Did you actually watch *Frida* or did you only NetFlix it so you could steal ideas from the Mexican interiors?

...Okay, my Beast, I am just back from India, and I mean literally walked into the loft ten minutes ago and you are the first person I had to "see." I know, I know, we've been e-mailing all the while I've been gone, but it's different back on home soil, y'know? As much as I adored the crazy bedlam of the bazaars and the *pietra dura* at the Taj and that lovely ochre-pink color of Jaipur, will you think the worst of me for admitting that I'm craving a huge, greasy, sloppy, 100% all-beef burger right this minute? It took every molecule of my willpower not to order the cabbie to drop me at Skyburger....

How could he not love a woman like that?

How could he have continued without wanting more than e-mails?

Ignoring the nagging thought that he might be sealing his doom, Tom closed the file and called up Isabel's last e-mail. He hit reply and began to type, stopped when he'd written a full page of drivel, then highlighted and deleted the entire mess.

He changed the subject line to CONFESSION. Advance warning, if Isabel was paying attention.

What to say, what to say? He stroked Polly's warm

fur and she preened beneath his hand, sinking her claws in the Navajo rug he'd thrown over the back of the couch so she wouldn't leave pinprick holes in the leather.

Isabel's heels had probably left dent marks in Rafe's chaise. Hot-cha-cha.

Grinning at the memories, Tom tapped the casing of the laptop. How would he tell Isabel that he was in love with her and had been for at least half the year, even before he saw her magazine picture with the wide laughing mouth and wild-woman hair?

Polly turned and blinked her golden eyes.

Right, Tom thought. Keep it simple, stupid.

To: IsabelParisi@NYletterbox.com
From: Tom@Gracenotes.biz
Subject: CONFESSION

Dearest Isabel:
It was me.

Love,
Tom

6

"HIYA, DARLING. Hey, princess," Isabel said, kissing cheeks with Natalie and Arianne at the door to her loft. The cold winter air clung to them, shooting a vivid memory of last night past Isabel's very ungirded defenses.

She'd crawled out of bed not twenty minutes ago, only to discover that Arianne had left a message on her answering machine requesting that they move the brunch up to eleven. After showering, she ran to the kitchen and started chopping spinach for a frittata, then raced around the loft to bring it to some semblance of order. Thankfully, the activity had kept her from thinking too much about her midnight sexcapade. Not to mention the nagging likelihood that she'd sent some sort of crazy e-mail to Tom about what had happened. The tune of an old Elton John song was still going round at the back of her brain.

"Morning, girlfriend." Natalie raised a paper bag from Balducci's. "Fresh bagels, the full assortment. Plain, poppy, onion, pumpernickel, sun-dried tomato."

"Bless you." Yesterday, Isabel had laid in a supply of farm-fresh eggs and smoked fish, but the bagels had to be as fresh as possible.

Arianne toted a net bag of oranges for the traditional mimosas. "Happy New Year, Iz."

"You, too." Isabel inspected her friend, as well-put-together as ever, even though it was immediately clear she was frazzled to the point of distraction. Despite the resolution to be spontaneous, the evening with Rafe must not have gone so well. Or perhaps too well? There was a suspicious puffy, tender look about Arianne's lips, even when she compressed them as if she was bursting with news.

Next, Isabel gave Natalie the once-over. *Well.* Although Nat's usual sparkle was dimmed, it was easy enough to read her face—and glowing cheeks. She had the look of a sexually satisfied woman. But the sadness in her red-rimmed eyes also meant she'd fallen hard, regardless of her resolution to the contrary.

Argh! Resolutions never worked.

Isabel suppressed a sigh. So much for revenge against Joe, the Disappearing Man. She only hoped that when this latest frog inevitably lost his luster, Natalie's optimistic little heart wouldn't break into too many pieces. Ditto for Arianne.

The three of them stood looking at one another, the silence taut with expectations and untold adventures.

Never mind, Isabel decided. A few mimosas would loosen their tongues.

She closed the elevator gate and pulled the heavy door shut. After locking up against vagrants since the downstairs door had been broken for ages, she turned, regarding her friends with a saucy grin. "Well, ladies. Looks like all three of us got a little somethin'-somethin' last night. But the question is, are we still single?"

"You bet!" Natalie said, trying to rouse some cheer.

Isabel wondered if the glint in Natalie's eyes was overly bright. *Uh-oh.* Did that mean Joe had pulled another vanishing act?

Arianne drew off her practical leather gloves and warm

hat. She shook frost out of her white-blond hair. "Yes, of course. Um, sort of."

Sort of? Isabel unwound an Hermès scarf from Natalie's neck and took her long wool coat, revealing a pair of skintight desert-colored camouflage jeans and a black Versace sweater. Typical of Nat, she'd dressed spiffily even for brunch with girlfriends, all the way down to vintage Fendi four-inch-heeled boots.

"You're both looking too good," Isabel said, stuffing their gear into the armoire that served as a closet in a loft devoid of interior walls. "Am I the only one with a hangover?"

That got a smile out of Arianne. "I didn't have the chance to overindulge." She quirked a brow. "Not in champagne, anyway."

"Natalie? You're so quiet."

Natalie, who was rarely quiet, grimaced. "Never mind me. I was up all night, so I'm barely awake."

Ah, Isabel liked the sound of that. This brunch could turn out to be rather illuminating.

She clapped her hands. "All right! Coffee first, then mimosas." She took the supplies and charged off to the kitchen, which was no more than a sink, an oven and a couple cubic feet of cabinet space. Two chrome restaurant-grade shelving units defined the area, along with an island made from an old wooden library card catalog now sporting chunky wheels.

Arianne and Natalie followed, exchanging a significant look. "Iz, have you got something to tell us about last night?"

"Oh, you know, just the usual." Isabel smoothed a palm over her breasts, hidden under a T-shirt, a fisherman's sweater and the hooded jacket she'd thrown on when the heat had failed to kick in. "I'm pleasantly tingly under all these layers. Whisker burn."

"I'll say." Arianne nodded. "I saw you sneaking up the ballroom steps with the man in the lion mask."

Natalie's eyes widened. "Do tell. Who was he? Did he bite?"

Isabel hesitated. She'd intended to stint on the details for a change, but what the hell, someone had to break the ice. Plus, her friends would think the sexcapade had actual meaning if she kept it to herself.

The way she wanted to.

Oh, damn!

"No biting," she blurted. "And I didn't get a name. But he sure knew how to give an oral."

They broke out into hoots and hand slaps, acting as bad as guys in a locker room. Isabel fell into habit and played the brash femme fatale for their amusement, boasting of her conquest. She got Natalie giggling and chiming in with bawdy comments, while Arianne alternated between disapproval and a certain envious longing.

She slid onto a bar stool, folding her hands beneath her chin. "Oh, Isabel. I worry about you. One of these days you're going to go off with the wrong man."

"Yeah," Natalie said. "One who doesn't know how to use his tongue." Her laughter died when she saw Isabel's somber expression. "Right, Iz?"

"Coffee," Isabel announced to forestall the questions that would come about her anonymous liaison. There weren't words to explain what had happened to her, and she wasn't looking forward to telling her friends that it was never going to happen again. They already thought she was too closed off to romantic possibilities.

She handed over their mugs and immediately dove for the minifridge under the counter. "You two go sit in the

living room. Give me ten minutes to get the food together.'' She refused their offers to help and shooed them
away.

Natalie and Arianne strolled to the living area that was
separated from the studio only by lengths of gauzy,
lustrous Indian fabrics hung from the conduits and pipes
left over from the building's era of industry. Two Bar-
celona chairs Isabel had recently bid on at auction on
Tom's recommendation were set up around a marble slab
coffee table with rough edges. There was a flokati rug
and an awful rump-sprung couch that barely passed as
shabby chic. She loved the contrast of flea-market goods
mixed with spare contemporary furnishings and was
working on Tom to sell her one of his floor model sofas
as a replacement. He'd said any time, if she was willing
to come by in person.

''Why is it so cold in here?'' Natalie called.

''Radiator's conked out again. I'll get the wrench and
give it a whack.''

''We'll use the blankets,'' Arianne said with Nordic
cheer as she pulled a chenille throw off the back of the
couch. They were used to roughing it at the loft, even
though Natalie was not-so-secretly appalled at Isabel's
thrift-shop wardrobe, and Arianne couldn't understand
spending savings on Chinese silk while subsisting on
cold leftovers of Chinese takeout.

Isabel banged on the radiator, loaded orange after orange into the electric juicer, quickly sliced and toasted
some of the bagels as the spinach frittata sizzled nearby.
Her intention was to make enough noise to prevent further questions about her masked encounter. But that also
meant she couldn't eavesdrop on her friends' quiet conversation.

''So,'' she said, going over with a tray laden with food.

"That party! Was it amazing, or what? The mansion looked fabulous and the crowd was so chichi I almost wished I was the fashion reporter instead of Nat." She peered down at the cluttered coffee table. "Want to shove the shoes and that other stuff off there, hon?"

Natalie picked up the sandals, took one look at their state of disgrace and cradled them to her chest like a mother with a sick baby. "You got these from Rafe?"

"Weird, huh?" Isabel set the tray on a stack of newspapers and art magazines. She shot a quick glance at Arianne, who was turning a pale shade of pink at the mention of Rafe's name. Definitely a little somethin'-somethin' going on there.

"Gimme." Isabel retrieved the Monticellos and dropped into a chair. "Look at these ridiculous heels. I'll break my ankle. And the ribbons. I must have tied them wrong because I couldn't figure out how to get them off again." She fiddled with the tangled satin streamers. "At first I thought I'd have to sleep in them. I almost resorted to cutting the knots—"

"No!" Natalie snatched one of the shoes. "You can't do that. Let me try."

"Hey, leggo my Monticellos." Laughing to hide her strange affection for Rafe's latest gift, Isabel wrestled the shoe away. She stuck the confounded things under the table, then knelt on a stack of floor pillows to distribute plates and napkin-wrapped utensils. "Let's dig in while the eggs are hot. I made an Italian frittata in honor of Lucia and Rafe."

Once they'd filled their plates, she looked at Natalie. Fashion was always a reliable distraction. "I didn't get to see either of you before you left the party. What was in your shoe box, Nat?"

Natalie smiled dreamily. "Black linen mules with

fuchsia and lime-green rhinestones. The heel's way too low, but otherwise they are so me." She wrinkled her nose. "A two-inch heel? What was Rafe thinking?"

"Maybe that you'd need sensible shoes to run away from a certain man chasing you?" Isabel suggested with a wink.

Natalie shrugged, apparently not ready to reveal the details of her evening. Or not planning to run, most likely.

Isabel glanced toward the couch. Arianne was staring under the table at the shoes, her thoughts miles away. "Don't tell me." Isabel pointed a fork, wondering how any woman as beautiful as Arianne could also be so practical. "You got another pair of boring black pumps."

Arianne blinked. "Not quite."

Natalie stopped midbite. "Mmph?" She quickly chewed and swallowed. "My, my. So what kind of shoes *did* you get?"

"Red."

"Red?" Natalie and Isabel said in unison.

"Very red. With high heels and crystal-beaded ankle straps." Arianne waved a hand. "I don't know what Rafe was thinking. They're not at all my taste!"

"Sounds like CFM shoes." Isabel flicked her tongue out to catch a dollop of cream cheese. "One guess what Rafe was thinking."

"I *know* how he thinks. The man's a womanizer. A playboy. A..." Arianne plunked her plate on the table. She'd only picked at her food. "Oh, God, what am I going to do?"

Isabel raised her brows. Was Arianne saying what it sounded like? Had she actually let loose long enough to sleep with Rafe?

Natalie had gone to sit on the couch. She gave Arianne

a squeeze. "Tell us about it. You look kind of thunder-struck."

"I guess I am stunned. The night was great. Magic." Arianne started to blush again, and Isabel knew that was all they were going to get on the details of Rafe's performance in bed. Damn.

"But with the shoes was an invitation to dinner to-night. What do you think?" Arianne looked at them with her wide blue eyes. "Do I go?"

"Yes," Isabel said immediately. Not because she was a romantic or anything. For Arianne.

Natalie had no such compunction. "Of course you go!"

Arianne was still hesitating. "But I don't have any-thing to wear."

"Pfft." Isabel waved a hand. "You have tons of beau-tiful clothes."

"They're all so dull and practical."

Natalie narrowed her eyes. "Aha. And you want to wow him."

Arianne nodded.

"If we were at my place, I could loan you a real knockout Dolce & Gabbana number I just bought. Bright blue, slashed down to here, crisscrossed with these peek-aboo slits—"

"Don't frighten the girl," Isabel said. "Arianne has to tease before she can taunt." She got to her feet. "I might have something that will work. I found a Fortuny dress at—"

Natalie jumped up. "We're not putting her in your rummage-sale chic."

"Oh, all right. There is a dress I've never worn. I had it made from a piece of gorgeous red silk, but there wasn't enough fabric so it's practically backless and gyno-exam short…''

In minutes, Natalie and Isabel came back from the bedroom area with a flirty cherry-red dress that looked no bigger than a handkerchief on a hanger. Arianne's eyes went round as she rubbed the slippery silk between her fingers. "I can't wear this."

"Sure you can."

"Rafe will die when he sees you in it," Natalie said, "but at least he'll go happy."

It took some fast talk and several changes; but they finally persuaded Arianne to take the red dress with her and *consider* wearing it to dinner tonight.

"I don't understand," Isabel said, getting frustrated. "You hinted that the sex was fantastic, so what's to hesitate over?"

"I told you. It's Rafe's reputation. Love them and leave them…with a Tiffany box…" Arianne's voice faded. She shook her head, apparently overcome by the enormity of the situation.

Natalie jumped in. "This isn't just about sex, Iz, you dolt. It's Arianne's entire future. Some women expect intimacy to develop into a real relationship."

"Like you did with Joe, the Disappearing Man?" Isabel shot back. "No one would catch me mooning after a guy for an entire year."

"Or even a day," Arianne said dryly.

How wrong you are, Isabel thought as she downed a good third of her mimosa. But she would not apologize for herself.

Natalie glowered. "You don't know the first thing about Joe."

"Number One." Isabel raised a finger. "He has a penchant for running out on you."

"Yeah? Takes one to know one."

Isabel sputtered. Though she frowned at Natalie and Arianne, she knew she wasn't mad at either of her friends. They could only know as much about her as she gave them. And that was more than most, but still less than the truth.

Her stomach churned. The urge to check her e-mail for a calming, rational note from Tom was nearly overwhelming. He was the only person she'd let all the way past the walls she'd erected in defense of her miserable introduction to the male species.

"Please, let's not snipe at one another," Arianne said. "We all had eventful nights and our emotions are still running high. Remember, we became friends because we support each other in spite of our differences."

Isabel sank back onto her pile of pillows. "You're right."

Natalie offered a tentative smile. "Sorry."

"You don't have to apologize." After a moment of hesitation, Isabel crawled over and climbed up onto the couch, worming herself into the space between Natalie and Arianne. She sat with her knees drawn up to her chin, her Indian sari skirt folded over tattered leggings and thick wool socks. "I'm really not as heartless as I seem. It's all an act."

Arianne's expression was filled with affection and concern. "I know that, Iz. But maybe you need to pick out a guy and spend enough time with him so that *he* can learn that."

"You're always telling me that I give my heart too freely," Natalie said, "but you're the opposite. And that's so sad. We want you to find a true love."

Isabel's frown returned. Their words touched too close to the lonely, frightened girl hidden inside her.

She deliberately changed the subject by nudging Natalie with her elbow. "Speaking of true love, you haven't told us what happened with Joe. Did you go through with the plan to pretend not to recognize him?" Isabel laughed, even though it was highly unlikely that Natalie had pulled off the deed without surrendering her heart all over again. "I'd have loved to see the look on his face when you gave him tit for tat and sashayed out of his life."

Natalie searched for words. "Well..."

Arianne rolled her eyes. "Boy, do we ever need to stop asking Isabel for advice. She told *me* to do a striptease on Rafe's bar."

Natalie groaned. "After what happened with Joe, I might have preferred the striptease."

"Oh, no, Nat. What did you do?" But Isabel knew the answer based on the redhead's kicked-puppy look.

"It's what I didn't do that's the problem." Natalie leaned back, blinking away the moisture in her eyes. "He tried to apologize, but I wouldn't let him. You know how I am. I never could hold a grudge. I left without saying anything, so I guess that's that, huh?"

"It doesn't have to be," Arianne said sympathetically. "You could talk to him. See where it leads."

"And say what? Hi, it's me. The woman in the gold mask. Remember? We danced the horizontal mambo until four a.m. and I think I'm in love with you? Oh, and by the way, can I have my mask back, please?"

There seemed to be no answer for that.

Isabel took a breath. "Okay, so the payback didn't work out the way you'd hoped. But you still got laid." She grinned, trying to take the misery off Nat's face. "I'd call that a successful night."

Natalie tucked a strand of shiny hair behind her ear. "You'd call that a successful first date."

They all laughed, though the merriment soon degenerated into sighs. Then silence.

"So here we sit," Arianne announced after a while. "A blonde, a brunette and a redhead."

Natalie resumed her brave smile. "Still single on New Year's Day."

Isabel threw her arms around them. "But very well screwed."

7

ISABEL RAN OVER to her desk as soon as Arianne and Natalie had departed, resupplied with hugs and kisses and encouragement to embrace their inner wild women in whatever manner suited them. Stripteases and one-night stands might not be the right choices, but Isabel was sure they'd find their own way. To love, if that was what they wanted.

Arianne had bravely vowed to attend Rafe's dinner in the red silk dress, though she'd drawn the line at promising more.

Natalie was also on her way to Rafe's mansion for an exclusive interview. She was a trouper, carrying on even though she was smarting. If her Joe was a mensch, he'd wake up to what a great gal Nat was and start *chasing* her for a change.

Isabel was the only one without prospects. Of course, her masked lover did know her name, so there was some possibility that he'd engage in a little chasing of his own.

Unlike Natalie, Isabel was hoping that wouldn't happen.

What had Nat said? *We want you to find true love...*

Isabel sat at the desk, feeling twittery inside. It was strange, but when she thought of true love, the image that came to her wasn't a man in a gilded lion's mask, but an indistinct figure...

A man at a drafting table, with a computer nearby.

Even though he was faceless, she knew him well enough to recognize that he was the one for her.

Tom Grace.

Gah! Isabel banged a fist on the desktop. Too much female bonding was making her soft. She could not be in love with Tom for the simple reason that he knew too much about her.

She pulled the laptop over and tapped keys until she found a copy of the e-mail she'd stupidly mailed to Tom after she'd gotten home from the Venetian ball. It was a mess, but the meaning was clear enough. Now Tom *really* knew too much about her. Even—she gulped—about her encounter with a stranger. Had she purposely sabotaged her relationship with Tom by giving him details that would change the way he thought of her?

Her face flaming, Isabel checked her incoming mail. She dreaded what Tom would write, although he'd never been anything but warm and understanding in the past.

Her gaze flew across the spam glutting her electronic mailbox and lit on a letter from Tom's address. Subject: CONFESSION.

Suddenly there was a chunk of ice in the pit of her stomach. With numb fingers, she clicked Read.

And she read.

All of three words.

It was me.

THE SILENCE WAS OMINOUS.

Tom sat in his office at Grace Notes on the second day of the new year, wondering if it was possible for e-mail to be threateningly silent. If so, his was.

There'd been no response from Isabel.

He'd checked, and his ''confession'' had been delivered. A hundred times since then, he'd started to write a plea for forgiveness, explain that he'd been carried away by the moment, but he hadn't meant to hurt her, that she should give him a shot at proving how right they were for each other.

Every time, he'd stopped himself. She had to know what he wanted, which meant the next step was hers. He was willing to let her make it, but he'd thought she'd strike swiftly.

Instead...only silence.

A cold shoulder was far worse than anger.

He knew by experience. His well-to-do family had been mystified by his decision to become, as they put it, a carpenter. At least try architecture, his father, a renowned surgeon had said. Graces are professionals, his mother, administrator of a billion-dollar research center, had needlessly pointed out. Tom's older sister was also a doctor; his younger brother on the way to a Harvard MBA. But Tom had always liked wood, design, working with his hands. Though he'd gone to his father's ivy league alma mater as demanded, it had been to acquire a master's in Fine Arts.

After he'd cashed out his trust fund and started Grace Notes on a relative shoestring, he'd been given the disapproving cold shoulder at family affairs for at least a year. But he'd stuck to his guns, and eventually his parents had realized they were being prigs. Especially when their colleagues began asking how to acquire Grace Notes pieces and they realized he might not be such a failure after all, even though his baffled father continued to refer to his son as a longhaired hippie. Likewise, Tom thought the elder Graces were too rigid. Yet they had managed to accept each other for what they were.

How his family would react to a person like Isabel was anyone's guess.

In multiple e-mails, she'd teased him about his stuffy New England upbringing, asking him how he'd ever become friendly with a gutter rat like her. He saw the hurt behind her words, and while he'd once explained his theory that the best and most interesting people were the "beasts" of the world, she continued to make cracks about her low-class roots, being a mutt, how she'd had to fight for every snippet of respect and scrap of success that came her way.

No matter how many times he wrote it, she didn't seem to understand—with her heart—that he found her both admirable and inspirational.

And now he'd pushed too hard and scared her away.

Agitated, Tom got up from his desk and crossed to the drafting table positioned adjacent to the windows that overlooked the factory floor. Drawings were tacked to the work surface, but they held no interest for him.

What he'd returned to again and again, were the masks he'd kept after the party. His would have to be returned to the costume shop, but Isabel's was unique—an original concoction layered in red pinfeathers and embellished with white-and-black plumes. Both masks looked the worse for wear, hers with broken feathers and missing beads and crystals, his slightly crushed from—

Tom smiled. Well, *that* had been worth it.

A sharp whistle pierced through the constant clatter of the factory below. A smattering of male catcalls rang out above the whine of table saws.

Tom parted the wooden blinds to see what was happening out there.

Isabel was happening. She stopped briefly to ask one of the workmen for directions. Then, proud and brazen as a Valkyrie, she charged across the cement floor of the factory space, ignoring the workers' continued interest as

she made a beeline for the stairs that led up the short
tower that held the office and reception area. She wore a
fringed suede jacket with tall boots and tight jeans that
showed off every inch of her long legs as she strode
purposefully toward Tom's aerie. Her complexion was
stark, with high color in her cheeks and blazing eyes.
There was an odd bundle in her arms that he couldn't
identify.

The metal steps rattled as she leaped them two at a
time. Something large and exultant built inside Tom with
every clanging footstep.

Isabel was here. Isabel…Isabel…

Every worker on the factory floor had stopped and was
watching slack-jawed. Tools and packing cartons had
been abandoned. Safety goggles were shoved up for a
better view.

Tom's secretary stood at the top of the stairway. "Pardon me, miss—"

Isabel barreled by. "Where is he?"

"Just a minute, please," Janet said. "Do you have an
appointment?"

Tom opened his office door. "Never mind, Janet. I
know her."

Isabel's head snapped around. "You're Tom Grace?"

"The one and only," he said, standing tall for her
perusal.

The furniture makers who'd gathered at the bottom of
the office tower to watch began to murmur among themselves. Probably placing bets on Isabel's identity. Those
closest to Tom knew that his dates were minimal. Certainly no woman had ever come looking for him.

Tom waved at them. "Show's over. Get back to
work."

"Oh, no." Isabel threw the items in her arms at him. "The show is just beginning!"

Thud, thud. He looked down as the shoes hit his chest and fell to the floor, atop his crumpled tuxedo jacket. "What the hell?"

"I can't get them unknotted. Two days I've been trying and they're driving me mad." She came at him. "Same as you!"

He caught her arms. "Hold on, Isabel."

She stopped, breathing hard, her eyes wide and brilliant as she stared. He remembered that she was seeing him for the first time and felt himself growing warm as her gaze traveled across his face. Her expression was filled with a small percentage of wonder beneath the fire-spitting anger. That gave him hope. At least it wasn't disgust.

"You…" She seethed. She wrenched away and waved her arms. "You…*rat bastard.*"

Laughter from below. "You tell him, sweetheart."

"Sneaky, slippery, slimy sleazebag," she spat.

"I'm not that bad, am I?"

She cocked a hip. "Oh, yeah, you are."

"You can call me all the names you want." Isabel's hot emotions were exciting to Tom, though he was aware of the onlookers even if she didn't care what they overheard. "But let's go into my office." He nodded to the secretary. "Janet, hold my calls."

The motherly woman smiled encouragement. She thought he was too lonely and had made several unsuccessful attempts to set him up on blind dates.

Tom ushered Isabel inside. With a shrug for the whistles from the eavesdropping workers, he went back to scoop up the jacket and the tangle of the beribboned shoes. He recognized them from the New Year's Eve party.

"Ahem," said Janet as he was about to close the door.

Tom looked where she pointed. Isabel's lace thong trailed across the threshold of his office. Apparently it had fallen from the pocket of the tux.

Janet winked as he snatched up the revealing undergarment.

He slammed the door and hurriedly dropped the stuff on his desk before turning to Isabel. "I know you're mad."

She stood on the other side of the desk, her hands on her hips. "*Mad* doesn't begin to define what I'm feeling."

"Listen, I made a mistake. I should have told you who I was before we—" He gave his head a little shake. "My only excuse is that you were so persuasive. And irresistible."

"Oh, no, you don't. I'm not interested in your sweet talk. All of that, what happened at the party, that was a—a foul. It never happened. Your mistake was coming to the party in the first place!"

"No, that was the smartest risk I ever took."

"But it wasn't *your* risk to take. How many times have I told you that I didn't want us to meet?" She stalked around the office, flailing and fulminating.

He went to the windows that rimmed the office and closed the blinds one by one.

Isabel continued. "Oh, what an ego on you! Completely ignoring my wishes! Want to tell me why you thought it was your decision to make, huh?"

"Simple." He lifted his hands. "Because you were wrong."

She stopped. He could practically see the anger draining out of her. But she stubbornly crossed her arms and pooched out her lower lip. "*You* say."

"Isabel…" It was a joy to use her name. He almost smiled. "Isabel, for a smart woman, you can be so dense. All you have to think of is how it was between us in that alcove—"

She put up a hand. "Stop. That didn't happen."

"Is that how you dismiss all your one-night stands? Erase them from your mind?"

"Don't throw my past up to me," she warned. "I told you all that junk about myself in good faith. In confidence, I mean. You were supposed to stay—stay—" She gestured at his computer, then said with renewed heat, *"Out of my life."*

"Why?"

She hesitated. "I don't have to answer that."

"Sure. That would mean examining your motives." He approached her, and she hunched her shoulders up to her neck, drawing away from him although she didn't actually step out of range. "I understand that you don't feel safe with me being a real man who wants you in the real world, instead of some anonymous electronic blip on the computer screen."

She tilted her head forward, not looking at him. Her black lashes lowered. "You weren't anonymous."

"Close enough."

"Our friendship was real."

"Yeah, and that's not changing, no matter how many shoes you whip at me."

She breathed heavily, in and out, almost letting herself laugh. "Sorry, I guess. I just—I got so frustrated after I read your confession. I've been caged in my loft for the past twenty-four hours, pacing and worrying and cursing you and trying to undo those shoes so I could send them back to Rafe—''

''Why would you do that?''

A glance skimmed his face. ''I didn't want the reminder.''

''I'll take them, then. Even if they're the only part of you I get to keep.'' He touched her arm. ''Tell me that's not how it's going to be, Isabel.''

She threw her head back, full of umbrage and bravado. ''Why? You want another piece of me?''

He couldn't let her reduce their relationship to only sex.

''Yeah,'' he said, and his voice had gone all husky and rough. ''Yeah, I want a piece. Another piece of mail to join the hundred others in my Isabel file. A piece of the pumpkin pie you dole out on Thanksgiving day, to me and all the rest of your friends. Peace of mind, the kind a person gets when they know there's always going to be someone around to laugh with, gripe to and count on. Most of all…''

He put his arms around her. ''I want a piece of your heart, Isabel. And I'm greedy.'' He kissed her flushed cheek, hoping it was auspicious when she didn't pull away. ''I want the biggest piece you have to give.''

She squeezed her eyes shut. ''What if I don't have *any* to give?''

''I'd say you underestimate yourself.'' And that she'd had plenty of training in that from her cruel stepfather and a mother so weak she'd allow her daughter to be scarred by his vitriol and abuse.

Isabel blinked at him, then gave an awkward, mirthless laugh. ''You think you know me so well.''

''Oh, and you believe I don't?''

She tipped up her chin, narrowed her eyes. Leaned into

his chest. "Then tell me what's in my mind right now, why don't you?"

A certain heat was building between them. Her body had gone from brittle to lissome in his arms. By her rapid breathing and the way she wet her lips with a flick of her tongue, he had no trouble reading her mind. But sex wasn't the way he wanted to go. It was the wrong message when she already clung to the mistaken idea that her greatest value for men was in the pleasure she gave and received.

His body, though, had another reaction. And he could tell that she knew it. With an infinitesimal adjustment, her hip nudged his thighs, brushed his already-thickening arousal.

"You're thinking you can distract me," he said.

Her left arm was crushed against his chest. Lightly she touched her dangling hand to his fly, fingertips pattering maddeningly in a butterfly caress. His prick twitched, swelled. "Wrong. I'm thinking I already have."

Groan. "That proves nothing, Isabel."

"Except that it *is* sex you want from me," she whispered, trying to slip her fingers past his belt.

"No." He held her hand still. "I won't let you dismiss me that way."

"You had no complaints on New Year's Eve."

New Year's Eve—enough fantasy material to keep him going for years. But he gave her a blank look and said, "Uh, I don't remember that. What happened?"

"Oh, very funny."

He stroked her spine. "New Year's Eve wasn't only about sex for me. I know that's not what you want to hear, but it's the truth. I was making love. To you, Isabel Parisi, not to some anonymous hot, willing body that I rented for the night. That was why I wanted to see your face while it happened." He put his mouth near her ear. "Beauty."

She shivered. "Stop."

"Call me Beast."

"Too late. You're not the beast anymore."

"Then call me Tom. You haven't yet."

A silence welled until finally she parted her lips and said, "Tom," in the smallest voice possible, like a whisper of silk.

"Look at my face. What do you see?"

"No," she said, pressing her forehead against his shoulder.

He stroked between her shoulder blades, feeling the breath shuddering through her, then the tension as she gripped handfuls of his shirt and wrenched it open, popping buttons from their holes. Her fingers fanned across his ribs. Fire licked his senses despite his determination to make her see him for who he was.

"Wait," he said.

She opened her mouth and pressed her lips to his neck. "Kiss me."

Her throaty plea went through him like a hot blade cuts butter. Distantly, he was aware of the busy sounds of a manufacturing concern—a phone ringing, nail guns popping—and at the front of his mind was the knowledge that he was making another mistake. Except that Isabel, by her own account, rarely went back for seconds. That she'd come here knowing what might happen between them, had looked him in the eye and still couldn't stop her desire, was significant.

At least he hoped so. Because he was weak.

He kissed her.

IN MINUTES, they were all over each other, ripping off most of their clothing as if they were on fire. *Stupid,*

stupid, stupid, Isabel kept thinking, even while she sucked at Tom's tongue and tore off his shirt. With shaking fingers she reached inside his shorts and stroked every hesitation and damned thoughtful concern out of him. No man could actually think coherently when all blood had gone south, and the truth was that she was acting on little more than raw instinct herself.

She knew she wanted him, at this moment.

There was no afterward. No tomorrow. Hadn't been for years.

Except that Tom's touch lingered reverently. Even in their rush, he slowed and used his hands and his mouth, loving every inch of her, with his eyes searching hers out again and again, asking her questions she didn't want to comprehend, let alone answer.

She bit his shoulder. He caught her, holding her against him as he staggered forward and slammed her bare bottom onto the drafting table. She hitched herself up on the slanted surface, knocking the Venetian masks aside, crinkling his drawings. The wooden blinds on the window behind the desk clattered like bones.

She yelped when he shoved her top up to her neck and took a long tingling pull on her nipple, his teeth pressing into her flesh. "*Oooch.* Can they hear us?"

He put his hand across her lips. "Shhh."

She kissed his fingers, sucked on them when they curled into her mouth. Wasn't she supposed to be mad at him? This didn't seem like it. Or taste like it.

Tom was bound to get ideas, ideas like those Nat had spoken about—intimacy developing into a relationship.

Oh, yeah, this was stupid. *Stupid and risky.*

So then why had she started it?

Because she wanted to be stupid and risky, in the biggest, most stupid, riskiest way of all? She wanted her life to be changed?

"Yes," she said, when he ripped open the packet he'd rescued from his wallet in the pants down around his ankles. Instead of giving him room, she pushed even closer against him, locking her legs around his waist so that as soon as he was sheathed there was nowhere to go but up inside her, all in one gloriously filling thrust that made her throw back her head and—

"Shhh," he said, kissing her.

She laughed against his puckered mouth. One of these days, they were going to do it where she could make as much noise as she wanted.

"Okay, I'll be as quiet as you." Deliberately, she tightened her inner muscles on his shaft, and he let loose with something that was halfway between a grunt and a shout.

His head reared back. A glint had come to his eyes. Six-packed abdomen rippling, he rocked into her, making the motion into one long spiral of pleasure that twisted in on itself and then widened and rose higher and curled tighter and tighter and tighter....

The drafting table knocked rhythmically against the window ledge. She squeezed his waist between her thighs, squeezed down even harder on the shriek building inside her.

Instead she crooned. "C'mon, c'mon. Give it to me..."

"You," he said, still rocking, "you give it to me. Tell me what I want to hear."

She shook her head. Mystified.

His pumping slowed, when she wanted him to speed up.

"I don't know!" she blurted.

"Tell me."

"No."

He took her chin in his hand and tried to make her look at him. She remembered his eyes best of all. Dark brown and bottomless. She only dared one glance. *"Tell me,"* he said.

"Damn you."

"Isabel…"

She closed her eyes, refusing the emotion inside her.

"All right," he said, and started to withdraw.

Her thighs tightened, keeping him close. "What do you think you're doing?"

"Using sex to make us close, just the way you use it to distance yourself. But if you can't handle—"

"Th-that doesn't make sense."

"You're the one who invented this game."

She moaned. *"Tom-m-m-m."*

"A name," he muttered, sliding deeper again. "That's progress. Maybe next you can look at me."

Her eyes opened. She stared at him, full on.

"What do you see?"

She shook her head, still uncertain.

He thrust, breaking the dam inside her so she came, shuddering, in what felt like a molten river. There was the rush of sensation and the hurtful pressure on her constrained heart and then there was something more, something indefinable.

"I'm your lover, Isabel," Tom whispered as he laid her down on the drafting table. "Your lover," he said, grinding against her with a sharp, exquisite contact that renewed her pleasure tenfold. He sighed, his hands on her hips, his torso arching away from her as he was wracked with his own climax. The force and intensity of it was evident on his face. Incredible. Alarming. And still his voice rose, expanded, filling every questioning space in her head. *"Your lover."*

8

To: Tom@Gracenotes.biz
From: IsabelParisi@NYletterbox.com
Subject: I can't

I'm sorry for running out on you again at your office yesterday, but you know I had to do it. I'll be blunt, Tom. I can't be the person you want me to be. You're sweet and good and, well, an incredible lover to put it mildly, but this is as far as we go. Never thought I'd be so clichéd, but here it is: It's not you, it's me.

I have a damaged heart. For a long time, I thought I was dead inside, but now I know I'm not. Thanks to you, Tom. You gave me that, and I'll never stop being grateful.

But when I woke up this morning, still thinking about what happened in your office and what you wanted from me, I knew that it wasn't going to work. You need a good, decent woman who can love you all the way, without being slowed by the heavy baggage I'm lugging around. Maybe if I go into therapy and finally deal with my self-esteem issues—oh, God, can you believe this? I am such a freaking cliché!!!

Still. There can't be any maybes, Tom. We're over.

You're a friend, and, yes, you were my lover. For a few beautiful moments. I hope that's enough.

XOXOXOX,
Isabel

To: IsabelParisi@NYletterbox.com
From: Tom@Gracenotes.biz
Subject: Yes You Can

My beauty, Isabel: You think that after you I could ever be satisfied with a *good* woman? Not a chance.

Love,
Tom

P.S. I'm through with e-mail. From now on, we talk in person. You and me, one on one. Get ready because I'm coming over to tell you what's enough.

To: Tom@Gracenotes.biz
From: IsabelParisi@NYletterbox.com
Subject: re: Yes You Can

NO, Tom. Don't bother. I won't let you in.
I mean it.

Iz

But did she mean it?

Damn. Isabel practically tossed her laptop across the surface of her worktable, rumpling the length of white silk she'd laid out in hopes of getting some work done on the patterns she'd been experimenting with before her sham of a love life took precedence. She'd written a dozen variations of her letter to Tom throughout the day, shoveling in the clichés and psychobabble when it really did come down to just one big old gigantic flaw.

Her. She was a mess of a person.

Her friends knew it, but they were tolerant. And they didn't have to live with her. Have sex-equals-intimacy with her. That was the relationship killer, right there.

And she couldn't be around Tom *without* it.

She knew he wouldn't obey her last e-mail, even if he got it. Although she'd opened his response not that long after he'd sent it, she was guessing that he was already on his way, charging into the fray with the purest of hearts.

Bless him. He deserved the best, and that wasn't her. He'd see that, eventually.

She capped her bottles of fabric dye, thinking about what underwear she'd put on that morning. Raggedy-ass mismatched Calvin Klein. And she hadn't shaved her legs since New Year's Eve.

She reached a hand to her calf. A few pinpricks of stubble. Not good enough.

Was there time to eat an onion?

Oh, for God's sake, she was losing it. All she needed to do was be sure the door was locked.

She was standing by the elevator door when she heard the familiar rumbling wheeze of its ascent. Tom? Already? He must have helicoptered in from Brooklyn. Why hadn't her landlord fixed that downstairs lock the first hundred times she'd asked?

Okay, Tom could come up, but he still wasn't getting in. Panic fluttering in her belly, she rolled back the steel-barred industrial door to check the shaft. Damn, the elevator was already closer than she thought. Two floors away.

She was sliding the door closed again when the top of the elevator appeared, shaking and groaning ominously. Worried that it was breaking down, she stopped to check through the gap only to see that it was Tom making the noise. His hands were fisted on the rusty iron gate, rattling it like a prisoner gone mad as he shouted her name, "Isabel! Isabel!"

The elevator rumbled to a stop. They stared at each other for a moment before both suddenly realized that there was nothing keeping them apart. Tom threw open the accordion metal gate at the same time she shoved her door shut, clapping on the heavy-duty lock and chain that secured it.

Tom pounded on the door. "Isabel, you have to talk to me."

"No, I don't!"

"Let me in." He was tugging on the handle, making the casters shudder, but the lock held.

"Go a-*way*," she yelled, pressing her hands over her ears as she backed off. She sped through the loft, flipping past the hanging fabrics to reach the big queen-size bed angled into the farthest corner.

Tom was calling for her.

"I can't hear you," she bellowed, and dove into the bed, thrusting her head under the pillow like a child. A hundred thousand times, she'd done the same as a girl, hoping she could shut out the sounds of her rampaging stepfather.

"Can't hear you, can't hear you," she whispered into the claustrophobic bulk of the pillow. She tugged it tighter around her ears, muffling even her breath. There had even been times she'd hoped to smother herself, thinking with a child's simplicity, *"Then they'll be sorry,"* although deep down she'd known that her loss would be unremarkable in the world.

Suddenly she threw off the pillow. What was she doing? Tom was offering her the *opposite* of what she used to run from.

She gulped air, raising her head to listen for his voice. And heard only the hammering of her own heart.

She sat up. Put her head in her hands. All the fight was gone from her body.

What was that lyric again? *Someone changed my*—no, that was wrong, she suddenly realized. It was *saved my life*.

Tom had saved her. Her life was already changed. Now all she had to do was accept him into it.

But that was too scary.

Except...hadn't she, already? He'd been with her for the past year.

"No, no," she muttered. "E-mail doesn't count."

Anyway, it sounded as thought he was gone. She pushed off the bed and slowly moved toward the elevator door. Utter silence.

She let out a hiccupy sob. *You blew it, Iz.*

Then she heard a sound. A sort of metallic clang. And knocking. Not at the door. The window.

Fire escape.

Elation grew to immense proportions inside her.

Tap, tap, tap. Tom's voice called to her. "Isabel..."

She covered her mouth with her hand, holding in the cry of joy that begged to be released. Her entire body shook.

"Dammit, Isabel."

She took a deep breath and moved toward the window. Tom pounded on the glass.

She stopped, staring at him through wide eyes. A security grate was pulled across the window, but she could still see his face. He was speaking, begging, but she barely heard as she was propelled forward.

With fumbling nervousness, she unlocked the grate and pulled it back. Tom's fist stopped pounding. His fingers spread on the windowpane, and she thought of the wonder of having them touch her cheek. He would never hurt her. She could trust that.

With a sob, she threw open the window. Cold gusts of air billowed the panels of fabric hanging from the ceiling. Tom climbed inside. A light snow swirled around his shoulders, misting him with specks of ash and sparkling frost.

His boots stamped on her wood floor. "Isabel."

"I—" She stopped.

He was holding her Monticello sandals, with the satin ribbons like new again—unknotted and unwrinkled, spilling from his fingers in glorious, festive colors.

Okay, so he knew how to untie a knot.

Perhaps even the ones inside her.

She blinked back tears, but they wouldn't comply.

"Face to face, honey," he said, coming to stand before her. He put a fingertip beneath her chin and tipped it up. "Tell me what you see."

A tear rolled down her cheek. "My lover."

"Yes." His eyes darkened. "And my face?"

"I—" She sniffled, shook her head.

"I'm not exactly handsome," he said. "Can you live with that?"

Comprehension struck at last, even though it was unbelievable that Tom should have worried that he wasn't good enough for her. "But you're wonderful!" she cried. "You're magnificent!"

"Look again, Isabel."

She looked. Well…perhaps he wasn't movie-star handsome. His mouth was wonderful and the deep dimples and grooves that bracketed it told her he was a man

who laughed a lot. But his face was craggy and he did
have a rather large nose, and maybe his hairline was re-
ceding the slightest bit.

He was Tom, though. That was all that mattered to
her. Why would she wish for more when his eyes were
the kindest she'd ever looked into? He had character and
soul and, oh, the truth was that she believed with all her
heart that he was the most beautiful man on the face of
the earth.

"I love you," she said, giving the stupendous statement no thought at all because somewhere along the way
the knowledge had become a part of her. "I want to look
into your face for the rest of my life." She smiled, study-
ing him through glittering tears. "Didn't you know,
Tom? All along, it was me who was the beast."

He smiled. "You're blind."

"No. I'm finally seeing clearly."

"Ah, Beauty."

She crossed her arms, shivering in the cold air. "I honestly can't say for sure that I can do this, Tom. But, I
don't know, maybe we should...try."

"That's all I ask." He stepped toward her and wrapped
his arms around her, bringing her feet off the floor. A
few big strides brought them to the bed, and he set her
down on the end of it, dropping to his knees at her stock-
ing-clad feet.

She drew one up beneath her. "Now what are you
doing?"

He shook the sandals, arranging the streamers. "This
loft is drafty and the floors are cold."

"We could close the window."

"Yeah, but you need to wear shoes around the house."

"Not the Monticellos. I'd break my neck."

"I like these shoes. They put you in my arms." He'd

slipped off her sock, fitted the slender slipper onto her foot and was unerringly winding and weaving the ribbons into the proper crisscross pattern. He knotted and tied a bow.

"I hope you're planning on sticking around," Isabel joked. "Because these shoes are like mazes. I can get in them, but not out."

Tom had coaxed her other foot out from beneath her and was finishing with the second sandal. "I'll be here." He gave her leg a warm squeeze, then looked up as he tied a bow with deft fingers. "Will you?"

She swallowed. "Well, for sure I can't run in these shoes."

"Then I'll put them on you every time we make love and you start getting that panicky look in your eyes." He kissed her kneecaps and slowly crawled upward. "Because you're never running out on me after sex again."

She fell back onto the bed, loving the feel of his long, lean body covering her in warmth. "We don't need the shoes for that." There was a nervous little fillip of fear dancing around inside her, but she concentrated on Tom's eyes and soon enough it went away.

"All you have to do," she said, lifting her face to meet his, "is hold on tight."

And then his arms wound around her, and his kiss was on her lips, so solid, sure and abundant that she finally understood. Through all these years of blind desperation, what she'd been running toward was love.

TANTALIZING
Nancy Warren

1

ARIANNE SORENSON SMOOTHED the long black designer dress she'd purchased at last year's after-Christmas sale. By also using a promotional coupon, she'd received an extra ten percent off the already half-price dress, which meant that the actual total had only made her queasy, not truly sick.

She got into the cab which already contained Isabel and Natalie, and fastened her seat belt.

"I can't believe we're all still single," she said after swapping hello kisses with her "dates." "Why are we going back?"

"I get lucky every year," Isabel reminded them both. "I like to bring in the new year with a bang."

"I go for the shoes," Natalie said. "You know what those babies retail for?"

Arianne shuddered. "Don't remind me. I added up the cost of this party in shoes alone once and I swear you could buy a place in the Hamptons."

Natalie stretched her legs out and wiggled her toes. "I'd rather have the shoes. And maybe this year, Rafe will let me interview him. How about you, Arianne? What do you come back for?"

"Rafe." She said it without thinking, and both her friends stared at her. She blinked. "I'm his accountant. It would be rude for me not to accept his invitation."

The two still stared.

"What? You don't seriously think Rafe would look twice at me, do you? Have you seen the women he..." She tried to come up with an appropriate verb for what Rafe actually did with the endless string of women on his arm. She knew he took them to the best restaurants, the hottest clubs, the plays, even dragged them to the opera.

"Dates." She finally came up with the most encompassing word, though it seemed a feeble way to describe the process. One thing she knew, and was as predictable as pristine white snow was followed by brown slush, was that an affair with Rafe ended with a parting gift from Tiffany's.

"Of course he'd look at you. You're gorgeous." Nat said. "Right, Iz?"

"Sure, you've got that total Swedish ice princess thing happening. Rafe probably wants to melt you with his hot Italian blood."

For a second she allowed the image of Rafe and herself entwined naked on a dreamy-looking bed somewhere and was startled by the heat the thought produced in her belly. His skin was tawny, his hair black. The pale sunshine color of her hair was as close as sun ever came to her skin. Her skin was so fair she wore SPF 45 sunscreen all year round. How white her limbs would look next to his darker ones.

Contrasts. So many contrasts.

His family was from the hot and summery south of Italy, hers from cold northern Scandinavia. His nature was impulsive and generous, hers cautious and restrained.

He loved women in a casual, shallow way. They flitted

in and out of his life like so many dazzling butterflies. Arianne didn't love easily. And when she did, it went deep.

"I should just go home. I'm not in the party mood," she said as the cab drew closer to their destination.

"You have to party. We made a pact," Isabel reminded her.

"Hey," Natalie said, putting a hand on her arm. "Something's up with you. What gives?"

She debated not telling them, but they were her best friends, so she sighed and opened her evening bag.

She wasn't one of those women who had nothing but a tissue, a lipstick and her house keys in her evening bag. Arianne bought them large enough to squeeze her wallet inside. She liked knowing where her driver's license and credit cards were at all times.

She withdrew her wallet and flipped it open to the half a dozen photo sleeves. She took a quick glance at the picture of the little bundle of pink-and-white with the tiny mouth pursed in sleep and passed it over.

"Cute kid," Natalie squinted in the dim light and handed it to Isabel. "Whose is it?"

"Charlie's. His Christmas card was late. I just got it in today's mail."

"Charlie, you-used-to-be-engaged-to Charlie?"

"Yes." She stared out the cab window at the brightly lit streets of Manhattan. "If I'd married him, that would be my baby."

"Since when do you want to be married to a guy living in some hick town in the Midwest?"

"He was transferred. He couldn't help it. We're still good friends, sometimes I wonder—"

"Honey, Charlie was *born* to live in a hick town in the Midwest. You weren't."

"Love isn't about geography."

"Oh, I don't know. Every time I see the Monticello mansion I fall in love with Rafe," Natalie teased.

Arianne laughed, put the photo back in her wallet and decided to get over herself. Isabel was right. This was a night to party. So her entire apartment could fit into Charlie's double garage, along with his snowblower and his ride-on lawn mower. So she might always be a godmother or an aunt and never a mother herself.

So, she might end up as a single career woman, so what?

"Masks," she reminded the others as their cab drew up to the mansion steps.

She dragged her plain black silk mask from her pocket and slipped it over her eyes.

Isabel's mask was handmade and as wild as its wearer—an extravagant concoction of glitz, feathers and trailing satin ribbons.

Natalie's was gold satin bordered in matching sequins with a plume of gold feathers. It coordinated with her gold-beaded dress, which was so lethally short, Arianne asked, "Have you got gold panties on under there?"

With a wicked smile, Nat whipped up her dress, revealing a gold-beaded thong. Figured.

"Arianne." Isabel put a hand on her arm. "You've got to lighten up, girlfriend. This is a party. Drink some champagne, have some fun, go wild."

Natalie nodded, her gold feathers flapping like an extremely expensive bird's wing. "She's right. Life doesn't always have to be serious. This is a night to let loose. Behind a mask, you can be anyone you want."

"Or have anyone you want," Iz insisted.

In the bustle of getting out of the cab, she didn't have to answer.

They trod up the steps, three single New York women, a blonde, a brunette and a redhead. Just the sort of trio Rafe enjoyed welcoming.

The party was in full swing when they arrived. Once their invitations had been checked and they'd handed their coats to an attendant, they hovered together.

It always took Arianne a minute or so to adjust. The place was like something out of a fairy tale. Old and grand, it had been built in the gilded age by an industrialist who wanted to show off his wealth. Opulence was everywhere, in gilt sconces and antique Venetian mirrors. The floor was rose Carrera marble, stripped out of an Italian castle and brought over to America especially for the ballroom. The domed thirty-foot ceiling was painted in the Renaissance style with pink-cheeked cherubs and gauze-draped angels floating against a cloudy blue sky. She never tired of gazing at it.

For her friends to be back this year was a no-brainer. Isabel was at her most hedonistic during the holidays. For her, Rafe's party was like an all-you-can-eat-boy-toy buffet. Nat was here for the shoes and the fashion. But Arianne was damned if she knew why she was here.

She told herself she came because it was politic to schmooze with the man who had helped her rise in her accounting firm. But she knew Rafe didn't want to be schmoozed at his own party—besides, there were plenty of other women schmoozing and doing God only knew what else whenever he was around.

No. She hadn't come for that.

She didn't have Natalie's passion for shoes, either, though it was undeniably nice to have a new pair of very expensive, very chic black shoes every year. On the RSVP, each party guest was asked to give their shoe size. Arianne always added her color preference—black. It was the most sensible color and allowed her to get more wear out of the shoes.

But shoes alone weren't enough to draw her. She didn't want to have sex with a stranger, either, which was Isabel's thing. However, Arianne was beginning to wonder if the hollow ache in her stomach had more to do with sex than shoes.

Somehow, walking into that ball was like walking into a fairy tale. The setting inspired high expectations as though the prince would dance with her, and the shoes she'd leave with would be glass.

How pathetic was that!

At that moment she glanced up and caught Rafe, stunning in a tux, and the only person not wearing a mask, watching her. He told anyone who asked that since he hosted the Venetian ball, it would be inappropriate of him to wear a disguise

Arianne had no idea if that was his true reason, but his face appeared startlingly naked in a sea of masks. He drew her gaze, and she was more than usually aware of the sensuous features that made up his face.

His hair was blacker than a cave at midnight, his eyes only a shade lighter. Dark as bitter chocolate. His skin was tawny as though he'd just stepped out of the Tuscan sun, though Arianne knew he'd been born right here in New York.

He was tall and the extreme sports he indulged in kept his physique in top shape.

She sighed. No wonder women were drawn to him like flies to flypaper. He was rich, successful, young and gorgeous. The two blondes flanking him at the moment were a matched set, like his gold cuff links.

Seeing what her friend was staring at, Isabel said, ''You've worked for him for two years. How come you haven't worked late and ended up in bed?''

SHE SHOOK HER HEAD. "I would never mix business with pleasure. It's totally unprofessional."

Also, Rafe had never made any move suggesting they be anything other than colleagues, though for some reason she didn't feel like sharing that with her friends.

"I don't know," Isabel said. "The way he looks at you, I don't think he's thinking about debits and credits."

"Nonsense. He looks at every woman that way. It's called Italian charm. A major component of the Monticello gene pool."

"He doesn't look at me that way. If he did, I'd ask for a personal tour of his bedroom."

"Maybe he's just not interested in one-night stands."

Isabel turned away, and Arianne thought she saw a flicker of hurt in her friend's eyes. Maybe it had been a tacky thing to say, but Isabel was the first to admit her idea of a long-term relationship was breakfast together the next morning. Rafe might be casual, but he wasn't that casual.

And she hated even to admit to the sharp flash of…irritation she'd experienced at the idea of Rafe and Isabel sharing intimacies.

Natalie, who'd been gazing around the room idly, suddenly gasped. Beneath her gold mask her skin paled.

"What is it?" the other two asked in unison.

Nat swallowed and shook her head. "I thought I saw

someone I used to know. I was wrong." She forced a smile, but even through the mask her eyes glittered oddly. In a bright voice she said, "Look, Rafe's coming this way."

And so he was. Alone. He'd escaped from the pair of blondes—ditched them so politely, no doubt, they didn't realize they'd been ditched.

"He's sexy as hell," Isabel whispered.

"He's a womanizing playboy," Arianne reminded her friend, topping up her own memory bank at the same time.

"Hey," he said when he was close enough to be heard. He might look like the embodiment of a fairy-tale prince, but his conversation was modern American male.

He didn't even do the Italian double-cheek-kissing thing.

"Hi, Rafe," Natalie said.

Isabel made a quick scan of the ballroom before turning to greet their host. "Ciao, bello!" She flung her arms around him and gave a lusty squeeze. "Another fabulous party. Bigger crowd than last year, hmm?" She licked her lips in anticipation.

"More pairs of shoes being comped," Arianne said.

A flash of amusement showed in his expression. "You're always counting the cost, Arianne."

Something about his tone made her think he wasn't just talking about money. So she was a careful woman. She wasn't going to apologize for the fact.

"Someone has to," she reminded him tartly. "You'd bankrupt yourself on Tiffany's trinkets alone if I didn't keep an eye on things."

The gleam of amusement became more pronounced. "Ah, but the pleasure I receive from…giving gifts is worth it. There are still things money can't buy, Arianne.''

''Like the love of a good woman?''

''Exactly.'' And what on earth was *that* supposed to mean? she wondered as she stared into his unmasked eyes, knowing hers were much less readable.

''Rafe,'' Nat interrupted the silent clash of gazes, ''who is that man over there in the black leather mask?''

Obligingly, Rafe turned and scanned the crowd. ''There must be fifty men out there in black masks. Could you be more specific?''

''It doesn't matter. There was a man I thought I recognized, but I think he's gone into another room.''

A waiter walked up at that moment to offer them flutes of champagne. Arianne's accountant brain shuddered at the extravagance even as her tongue quivered with delight when she tasted French champagne. Vintage, probably.

She caught his gaze on her, amusement once more crinkling his eyes in a disturbingly attractive way and she had the uncomfortable feeling he'd read her mind.

''What do you think? This is the nineteen-ninety vintage. I would have served the eighty-five, but there wasn't enough in the cellar.''

Since she refused to lie and pretend she hadn't been calculating how much this champagne cost when he knew damn well she had, she was stuck standing there, speechless. The other two were no help in rescuing her from being labeled a cheap spoilsport.

Isabel was already searching the crowd for single men who might be interested in a private party, and Nat...it was hard to tell what Nat was doing. Deep-breathing exercises maybe. She appeared to be on some whole other plane.

Which left Arianne standing with Rafe unable to come up with a single thing to say.

Usually they were friendly in a businesslike way, had been ever since they'd worked together on a charity event two years ago. He'd been a celebrity auctioneer as well as a major donor, and she'd been the event treasurer. They'd hit it off instantly. He'd enjoyed the challenge of driving up the bids, knowing it was for a good cause, and she'd been delighted to count and record the generous donations.

Shortly after, he'd transferred his personal business to the large international accounting firm that employed her, specifying he wanted Arianne assigned to his account.

She'd been flattered—was still flattered. It hadn't hurt her career at all, either.

In spite of his playboy reputation, she knew how hard he worked and respected his intelligence and business savvy. However, he played just as hard, and while she didn't much mind the heli-skiing, mountain climbing and scuba diving, she had less patience with the women.

But it wasn't her business. She tracked his expenses, raised her eyebrows sometimes and teased him whenever she felt like it.

She had the odd feeing sometimes that he enjoyed flaunting his extravagant girlfriend-gifts under her nose. Like the time he spent three thousand bucks on an ice-blue camisole he'd carted home from some fancy lingerie place in L.A. frequented by celebrities.

"For three thousand bucks you'd think they could include panties," she'd snapped.

"But that would be a waste," he'd taunted her. "And I know how much you hate waste."

Why was she thinking about that now? It was nothing to her if he bought ridiculously overpriced underwear for his women. She needed to get away from the disturbing thoughts his presence was generating.

"I haven't seen your mother," she said politely, firmly pushing thoughts of ice-blue camisoles from her mind. "Did she fly over for the party?"

Lucia Monticello spent long stretches of time in Milan in her design studio and overseeing production of her shoes. She was a perfectionist and a hard taskmaster, but she had enormous personal charm and inspired loyalty.

Her son had inherited his mother's flair for business, but, Arianne thought, not Lucia's passion for family. The only one who gave him a harder time than Arianne did about his disposable bimbos was his mother. She wanted grandchildren from her eldest son, and she wasn't subtle about it.

"Yes. Mother flew home in time for Christmas. She's around somewhere. I know she'll want to see you."

"I'd like to see her, too."

"There you are, Rafe. Wonderful party!" Arianne turned to see a good-looking, very distinguished man, perfectly recognizable in the tiniest mask she'd ever seen.

"Glad you could make it, Senator."

"Excuse me," Arianne said, making a smooth exit, knowing she added nothing to Rafe's consequence in the politician's eyes. Now, if she'd been one of the well-known actresses at the party, or a model, it would be different. But a woman whose biggest asset was her brain…

What was the matter with her tonight? She should be having fun, sipping expensive champagne, dancing, flirting. Why should she care what Rafe's fancy friends thought of her?

She walked away, disgusted with herself.

Isabel and Natalie had already melted away. She

caught sight of Isabel chatting up a man whose assets were clearly visible. He had a stone jaw and a torso suggested he bench-pressed tour buses to keep in shape. Definitely Isabel's type, she thought with a smile.

Natalie was nowhere to be seen. She'd seemed sort of odd a minute ago; maybe Arianne would try and find her.

She sipped her champagne as she wandered through the rooms. She knew a lot of the people present. Not everyone wore their masks. Some had the kind on sticks that you hold in front of your face.

Rafe's mother, gorgeous and exotic in dark red velvet, was in the main ballroom. Her mask was black silk and sported two silhouettes of shoes outlined in something sparkly. Could be rhinestones, but Arianne wouldn't be a bit surprised if they were diamonds. Vintage champagne for hundreds of guests, real diamonds on a costume mask—really, she was going to end up with an ulcer tonight.

Still, Lucia had worked hard all her life and earned her success. She was generous to her family, her friends, her staff and to charity. If she wanted to wear diamonds on her mask, she'd earned the privilege.

"Ah, Arianne, it is wonderful to see you." Lucia's eyes sparkled right along with the diamonds in her mask as she grabbed her and kissed her on both cheeks. Not air kisses, like most New Yorkers, but real loud smackers. *Smooch, smooch.* Arianne smelled her perfume, something heavy and exotic that she had made specially, and also a whiff of the Gitane cigarettes she insisted she couldn't give up in spite of repeated nagging from her doctor and her son.

"You look simple and elegant, as always," Rafe's mother said. Her fashionista's gaze was laser-sharp as it inspected Arianne from top to bottom. She could probably tell the dress was from last season as well as the Monticellos on her feet. "And those shoes? You like them?"

"They're wonderful."

Lucia nodded, agreeing. "And black. Always you choose black."

"It's the most practical color."

She laughed, a deep, husky full-bodied sound. "Nonsense. A Monticello is never practical." Arianne wasn't sure whether she referred to the shoes or the family members and decided it was true on either account.

"I'm not sure why Rafe hired me, Lucia. All I seem to do is spoil your fun."

"That's ridiculous, my dear. We need your sensible streak and we love you for it. Besides, without us, you'd wear nothing but pumps."

Another laugh shook Arianne at the truth of those words. "I'm sure I drive Rafe crazy."

"Of course you do, that's why you two work so well together." A glittering smile, almost as bright as the diamonds she wore, crossed the woman's face as if she were harboring a delicious secret.

3

Rafe watched his two favorite women in the world chatting together. He'd been amazed when his mother and Arianne hit it off almost immediately.

It was a case of complete opposites attracting each other.

He wished the same chemistry had worked with him and Arianne, but she was never more than friendly with him.

She was driving him crazy.

Her cool ice-princess beauty had appealed to him instantly but it had been easy enough to resist because, in his experience, a decent accountant was a whole lot tougher to find than a beautiful woman.

It hadn't been long, though, before he realized that what he felt for Arianne was different than what he felt for most women.

He enjoyed her company, her conversation, her smarts, her quick wit and considered her one of his few female friends. Within a month of her coming to work for him he'd felt she was the one. He'd known enough women in his time to recognize that what he felt for Arianne was more than fleeting attraction. He was Italian enough to believe in love at first sight.

He'd tried to send subtle signals that he was attracted to her, and she'd responded to him with the same excitement as though he were a numbered company. Her clueless rejection of him was only making him more determined to reach her.

Lately, he'd been obsessing about getting her into bed. Things were getting so bad that the sight of a calculator made him hard.

He watched her cool Scandinavian beauty beside his exotic mother's and shook his head at the mysteries of attraction. He'd been to Sweden for a sales trip followed by some Nordic ski racing, and Arianne reminded him of the country of her ancestors—cold, remote, dangerous, damn near inaccessible and breathtakingly beautiful.

He knew she could be warm and funny, but her natural element was ice. Just as his was fire. He considered them a perfect combination.

He threaded his way through the partying crowd to his mother and Arianne.

"What are you two grinning about?"

"We were talking about how foolish you and I are, and how much we both need Arianne to keep us in line."

"I never said you were foolish," Arianne protested.

"Well, we are. Aren't we, Rafael?" his mother said, tapping his cheek. She then turned to look at Arianne. "But you know, my dear, a little foolishness would be good for you, too."

At that moment an older man approached Rafe's mother, lifted her hand to kiss it passionately and broke into a spate of Italian.

Since his mother's endless admirers got on Rafe's nerves in direct proportion to their bombast, he felt the urge to escape.

"Come on," he said. "Let's get out of the passion zone." He led her away.

A waiter offered a tray of champagne and Rafe took

Arianne's empty glass from her and handed her a full one before taking one for himself.

His companion frowned as she sipped.

"Something wrong with the champagne?"

She shook her head. "What is with everyone tonight commenting on how practical I am? First Isabel and Nat, then you, now your mother? What did you tell her about me?"

"Nothing. She's got eyes and ears, Arianne. She figured it out."

She felt blustery and annoyed as she sipped her champagne. Her vintage French champagne. "Well, there's nothing wrong with being practical. If more people in this world thought things through before they acted, the world would be a better place."

He appeared to ponder her statement. "More organized, perhaps, but would it really be better? Some of my fondest memories involved something spontaneous."

"Hmm. You mean sex, I suppose."

His mouth quivered. "I didn't mean only sex, but what the hell is wrong with spontaneous sex?"

"Nothing. *Nothing.*"

"How do you know? Have you ever had any?"

She glanced around and lowered her voice. "Are you asking me if I've ever had sex? You think I'm…I'm…"

She couldn't even complete the sentence. Is that how she came across to people? Virginal? She definitely should have stayed home and watched old movie reruns. Reruns of long-dead band leaders ringing in forgotten New Years. She was a young, single, healthy woman living in one of the most exciting cities on earth, and the most exciting man she knew thought she was a virgin. Depression settled over her like a cloud of gnats, their invisible little teeth biting at her.

He snorted with laughter. "I meant spontaneous sex. Not that there's anything wrong with being a virgin. I used to be one myself."

It was her turn to snort. "Back around sixth grade." She was marginally mollified to discover he didn't think she was a virgin, just a really boring lover incapable of being impetuous.

Suddenly, it seemed very important to make him understand she was perfectly exciting in bed.

"Well, for your information, not that it's any of your business, I've had many spontaneous sexual encounters." *Hah, so take that,* she thought, tossing her head just a little.

He leaned closer, a carnal gleam in his eye, and whispered, "Name one."

Name one? She couldn't even dredge up a single sexual encounter that seemed outstanding in retrospect. She could barely recall any past lovers. Rafe's presence had scared all her memories away.

She took refuge in haughtiness. "Certainly not."

His laughter was light and teasing and unbearably sexy. "Come on. I dare you."

"This is completely inappropriate. I'm your employee."

"This is a party," he reminded her. "And you're my guest. I don't think you have any tales to tell."

She pulled out the first fantasy she could think of. "The ladies' dressing room. In Macy's. I was trying on lingerie and my...um, boyfriend became overcome with lust." Suddenly she imagined herself wearing a three-thousand-dollar ice-blue camisole and Rafe overcome with lust. The very idea caused heat waves to ripple across her skin and her breath to hitch.

"You were in the change room at Macy's, overcome

with lust. Then what happened?'' Was it her imagination
or had his tone just become huskier? It sounded soft,
erotic and a little smoky, and he was close enough to her
ear that his breath caressed her.

She swallowed. ''And then, he…followed me into the
change room and we, you know…''

''No. I don't know. You what? Strategized how to get
the best discount on the lingerie?''

Her eyes narrowed in a glare. ''I do occasionally think
of something other than money. We had sex. Right there
in the change room of Macy's.''

For a long moment he gazed at her, and she'd never
been so thankful for a mask. She felt the warmth of a
blush creep up her neck, not certain how much was the
embarrassment of having told such a tale to a man who
was supposed to be a business acquaintance and how
much was due to his nearness.

After a long, tense moment, he said, ''I don't believe
you.''

So she'd made it up. What was he going to do? Ask
Macy's?

''I have hidden depths,'' she informed him.

''Now that, I do believe.'' And, with an enigmatic
glance, he walked away.

She stared after him, at the lean grace of his body, so
elegant in the tuxedo, underneath so very animal.

And the way he'd looked at her, the words he'd spoken, it was almost as though…he might be interested.

In her.

Yet he decided that second to walk away from her.

Her lips thinned. Not spontaneous, huh? Too practical,
huh?

She was going to do something so spontaneous, so
impractical that from now on, when people in general—

and Rafe in particular—thought about Arianne Sorenson, *practical* would be the last word they'd use.

Dance music filled her ears, something with a salsa beat. Her blood began to pound to the same rhythm. She needed to do something daring, wild and risky.

Following the provocative sound, she wandered to the edge of the dance floor and soon saw that Isabel had ditched Mr. Muscles and was now dancing with a dusky-skinned man in a Mardi Gras mask. She was twined around him like ivy on a tree trunk.

Arianne stood at the edge of the dancing couples, eyes beaming into Isabel's back. Her Latin lover swung her around in the dance and even through the mask she noticed Isabel's eyes were wide open and blank with boredom. Didn't look like it was his lucky night.

Arianne signaled to her, then jerked her head, indicating they should meet at the back of the room. She eased away to a less crowded corner and waited. Iz didn't let her down and was there in a couple of minutes, minus her latest flirtation. She shed them like leaves in autumn.

"What's up?"

"I need to do something wild and unpredictable," she said, already wishing she'd gone out this week and bought a brand-new dress. Something in red or gold that showed lots of cleavage and lots of leg. And she wished for one ridiculous moment that she'd paid full price.

Isabel expelled such a gust of air that one of the tiny white feathers on her mask wafted free. "*You* want to do something wild and unpredictable?" She was gazing at Arianne as though she'd said her parents were barnyard animals. "Why? Not that I'm discouraging you, but why?"

"I just do. I'm tired of being practical. I'm making my New Year's resolution tonight. Right now. This second.

My resolution is to be spontaneous and fun." She nodded her head sharply. "And I'm starting tonight. I'm going to do something completely crazy."

Isabel patted her shoulder. "Sounds like a great plan. Go for it." She peered into Arianne's eyes. "Though I am wondering how much champagne you've drunk."

"It's not champagne. It's the new me." Arianne nodded once more, hard. She was so determined to follow her plan she was giving herself whiplash.

Iz cocked her head to one side. "Am I here to give permission?"

"No, you're here because I can't think of anything wild and crazy to do!" she wailed.

"Do what I do. Pick out the biggest jackhammer here, turn him on and go for a ride." Isabel bit back a teasing smile as she reached into her strapless red satin bodice. "Do you need some condoms? I tucked a couple in here for emergencies—"

Arianne grabbed Isabel's arm and dragged her practically into a wall where they wouldn't be overheard. "No, I don't want condoms. Sex is so…private. I want people to notice I've changed. I'm looking for something to do in public."

"Any people in particular?"

Dark-eyed devils that laughed at her and didn't even believe she'd ever had sex in the Macy's change room for one. "No. Just people."

"Well, that's easy. Have raunchy sex with a stranger and be very, very noisy. And do it where someone might see you." Iz gazed around and said, "The top of the bar would be good. It's not very wide, but you're pretty thin. Or you could climb up there and do a striptease."

"Are you kidding?"

Isabel just gazed at her with challenge, and Arianne suspected, pity in her gaze.

She blinked. The very idea of sex in public made her queasy. "Never mind. I shouldn't have pulled you away from your latest conquest."

"No problem. He wasn't a contender. I was getting bored merely dancing with the guy. I'd have needed a wake-up call if I actually had sex with him. Tonight I need a man with a little something extra." For a moment, Isabel looked serious, but then she measured a length with her hands. "Ten inches ought to do it."

"Happy hunting."

Isabel shrugged. Maybe I'll see you later—at the bar."

"Very funny," Arianne said, as Isabel laughed and walked away.

She'd go find Natalie. Maybe she had some better ideas.

As Arianne searched out her other friend, she noticed Rafe chatting up a minor soap opera star whose idea of a mask was pink sparkly cat's-eye glasses and whose dress was everything Arianne's wasn't. It had about a tenth the material, all of which sparkled with beads and probably cost ten times as much as Arianne's restrained black. And she was pretty sure God had no hand in the making of those boobs. She resisted the urge to roll her eyes.

Rafe caught her staring and sent her a grin that had *don't believe you did it in the change room* all over it.

She glanced at his current lady friend and then back at him, making her eyes huge and blinking them like a total ditz. Honestly, for a smart guy, why did he always surround himself with such high-maintenance…flibbertigibbets. She grinned to herself. That was a grandmother word, but it fit. "Flighty flibbertigibbets," she muttered to herself as she stopped to exchange greetings with one of the Monticello vice presidents.

The man looked delighted to see her, and her squashed feathers opened a little until she recalled he was the vice president of finance. He was all excited to see her because she was as fiscally prudent as he.

Correction, as she was at work. This was a party, and here she was wild, spontaneous, fun, fun, fun.

She excused herself from the VP, knowing that this was a bad place to start being spontaneous.

Natalie. Must find Natalie.

But she was nowhere to be found. The evening was advancing and Arianne's reputation was still obnoxiously intact.

Oh, hell. Isabel was probably right. So she'd find a guy, have wild, noisy sex—but not too wild or noisy. In fact, maybe she'd be better to select a few possible candidates and plan an attack on Macy's for next week. With all the January sales on, she could probably have an orgy in the change room and no one would notice.

Her black Monticellos clacked across the marble floor with decision.

She could be as spontaneous as the next person. She just needed some time to plan it, that's all.

4

IF THE WOMAN WORE a larger mask, Rafe would start to wonder if that babe dancing and flirting with such determination was really Arianne.

But of course it was. Even if her mask had covered her entire face he'd have recognized the turn of her head, the way she stood, shoulders held back, her neck a long, fluid curve. Her breasts were small and perched high above a long waist, slight hips and endless legs.

Even her feet were long and slender. If ever a pair of feet were made for Monticellos, hers were. Not that he ever saw much of her feet or her legs. She tended to go for New York black. Dress pants, longish skirts and tonight's long dress. He'd love to see her in a short skirt and some color.

What he was going to see her in, if her behavior continued, was the arms of another man.

If he didn't want her so badly himself, he'd be chuckling at the way she was moving with determination from man to man. It looked as though she were trying to choose one and so far not finding any to her satisfaction.

He'd been joking with her when he challenged her, suggesting she'd never had spontaneous sex in her life. But it looked as if she was now determined to do just that. He should have kept his damn fool mouth shut.

And yet, if he'd done nothing else, he'd captured her attention and by bringing up the subject of sex between them, he wondered if he hadn't also raised the possibility of sex happening between *them* in Arianne's mind. And that had to be a first.

He kept an eye on her as he mingled with his guests, and he had the strong notion she had him in her sights, too.

Oh, yeah. He'd got her thinking all right.

She wasn't seeing him as her boss tonight, but as a man.

She might not realize it, but she was sending out little zinging signals to him. And he was responding with obnoxious speed.

I can be spontaneous, her behavior seemed to be saying. *Ping.*

His response was pretty clear. *Like hell. Pong.*

Now she was dancing as though her mission was to wear her shoes out in one night. *Okay, I'll show you. Ping.*

But he could see none of the guys she wrapped her arms around and gyrated with were doing it for her. *Not buying it. Pong.*

Here I am talking to other men. Attractive single men I might go to bed with, not even knowing their last names. Ping.

He crossed his arms and sent her a disbelieving grin. *Pong.*

Soon, very soon, he was going to take his own turn holding her in his arms on the dance floor. But for now, he was enjoying her antics too much to interfere.

What was she up to now? He finished dancing with the senator's wife and returned her to her husband, his gaze searching and finding Arianne, who was in the process of handing her business card to a shady-looking character Rafe doubted was even on the guest list. *Ping.*

And his move would be…

What the hell was he thinking? What was she thinking? It was one thing to dance and flirt, but if she started giving out her number…the hell with it. The game was over.

He strode toward her. Handing out her business card to some yokel was breaking the rules. *Enough.*

She appeared mildly startled, but not very surprised when he suddenly appeared in front of her. "You promised me a dance."

The lump of testosterone currently fingering her card as though it were her naked flesh didn't look nearly as complacent. Tough.

"Excuse us," Rafe said and slid his hand down her arm to catch her hand in his.

"When did I promise you a dance?" she asked coolly, as though unaware of the magnetic force field generated by their joined hands. He went a little light-headed as he contemplated what could happen if they joined completely. He glanced down at her, and she looked up at the same moment, her eyes the clearest blue like fine pale silk.

No, he decided. Not *if* they joined completely, the question was when.

"I was rescuing you from that deadbeat you were leading on."

Her eyes glittered colder. "I was not leading him on."

"You gave him your business card."

She sniffed. "He's three years behind on his income tax."

Rafe started to laugh. He couldn't help himself. "You're in the middle of a New Year's Eve party and you're talking to guys about their taxes?"

She couldn't quite restrain the quiver of humor that

disturbed the serenity of her expression like a tiny breeze over a still lake. She'd been playing him for a fool.

"You knew I was watching you."

She inclined her head and didn't deny his accusation.

They'd reached the dance floor and as they did, the orchestra struck up a waltz. He glanced toward the band and saw his mother step away, grab his uncle Georgio and join them on the floor.

He would have liked his first dance with Arianne to contain a little more bump and grind, but at least they were dancing. He slipped his arm around her waist and decided there was something pretty damned good about the waltz. She laid hers on his shoulder and with their other hands still clasped, they were off.

"You're a good dancer," she said after a minute, sounding far too surprised for his ego to be happy.

"Thanks. I've had a lot of practice. Italians have big families, and big weddings. I've danced at hundreds of weddings. You're good, too."

"I took ballroom dancing lessons right before prom."

Lessons hadn't taught her to anticipate his every move and nothing had taught either of them to move so effortlessly together. Beneath his hand he felt the shift and flow of her back muscles, the strength and suppleness of her spine. He didn't have to push and pull to guide her around the room, so he relaxed and enjoyed himself.

A woman who moved so gracefully and instinctively with him on the dance floor would be amazing in bed. Even as the thought occurred he forced it away before he embarrassed himself and her by getting an erection while dancing.

He tried to think about something else, but this close he could smell her light fragrance, see the color variations of platinum and gold in her pale hair.

There was a tiny chicken-pox scar to the left of her eyebrow on her otherwise flawless face.

"Arianne, you are so beautiful tonight."

She didn't answer with words, but he felt her body shift slightly closer. There was a lot of communication going on between them—more than words could express.

Maybe his compliment was shopworn, but she was beautiful tonight. More so than ever before. Through the slits in the mask, her eyes glinted with heat, like a hot spring under a frozen surface.

Her body temperature must be a couple of degrees lower than his, for her skin felt cool to the touch while he seemed to be burning.

They twirled a last time to the music, and he found himself short of breath. And it wasn't from the exertion of waltzing, but from the erotic sensations caused by holding this particular woman in his arms.

The music ended, yet he didn't let her go, but stared down at her as she held his gaze for a long, searching moment. He felt as though something momentous was taking place. Amid the noise and laugher, the music and the spilled champagne, the perfect food and perfect bodies, something new and imperfect was happening between him and Arianne.

His tux seemed stifling suddenly. He tried to think of what he wanted to say, how he wanted to phrase it. "Arianne, I…" But he couldn't find the words.

She broke the spell by stepping back and breaking eye contact. "That was great, Rafe. Thanks. I'll see you later." Then, while he stood there, Arianne all but sprinted out of range before he could articulate what he really wanted to say to her.

While he watched her go, he wondered. Now he'd finally seen beneath her cool professionalism to discover the woman inside. At last he knew she was as aware of him as a man as he was of her as a woman. What would happen next?

He cast a quick glance at his watch and blinked. Only ten minutes until midnight.

Hmm.

ARIANNE WET A TOWEL at the gold faucet and pressed it to her burning cheeks and the back of her neck. Something very peculiar was happening to her.

Rafe was... It seemed as though he wanted her.

Longing pulled at her belly. She'd always considered him as out of reach as a gorgeous movie actor on the screen. Tonight, however, he seemed to want her in the most basic way. One that had nothing to do with his finances.

Oh, how she wanted to respond. But he was...risky.

She pulled out her wallet and stared at the photo of Charlie's baby for a long moment. She could be living a pleasant suburban life right this minute. That baby, or one very like it, would be hers. She'd be a young wife and mother, shopping for sleepers, God help her, maybe even driving a minivan and going to bed with Charlie every night for the rest of her life.

She'd broken her engagement not because of geography, but because when it came right down to it, she realized she didn't love Charlie.

It would have been safe to marry him, as expected. Everyone from her parents to her friends had been shocked when she backed out of the engagement.

But she hadn't chosen the safe road when it had been offered her. She'd said no and taken the risk.

Damn it, living in New York, a woman alone, was a risk.

Being alive was a risk.

Spontaneous sex with an important client was closer to skydiving with no parachute than risky, but she couldn't think of a more dramatic way to demonstrate to Rafe and everyone that she was as much of a spontaneous risk taker as anyone.

She freshened her lipstick, took a deep breath and decided to jump.

The hell with the parachute.

According to her watch, there was five minutes until midnight. In fairy tales, the princesses ran away at midnight or turned back into drudges. In her version, the princess came into her woman's power at the stroke of twelve.

She straightened her mask in the mirror, enjoying the Mona Lisa curve of her lips. Rafe wanted spontaneous? He was going to get spontaneous, all right. Spontaneous combustion.

She strolled into the ballroom at three minutes to midnight and immediately searched for him.

Waiters were once more circling with champagne. Her excitement dimmed somewhat when she finally spotted Rafe in the middle of an animated group, far too many of whom were wearing skirts.

Well, she'd had her chance, hadn't she?

She shook her head when a waiter offered her a flute from a tray filled with glasses of champagne and glittering noisemakers. She didn't want champagne any more than she wanted to blow some garish paper-and-glitz horn.

Water would suit her mood better. And not sparkling water, either. Flat, tepid tap water. And instead of a noisemaker, a little contemplative silence.

She wandered to the bar set up at the back of the ballroom and had a painful moment of déjà vu. She'd done this same thing last year.

Of course, that's where she'd met Natalie and Isabel, so it had turned out great. A quick glance showed her no Isabel, no Natalie, no one at all at the bar. Everyone had moved forward for the big countdown.

"Water please," she said to the bartender, who brightened a bit when she plonked herself on a bar stool. Poor guy, it must be lonely back here.

Still, when he handed her the water, she rose again. She didn't want to end up necking with him just because it was New Year's Eve and only the two of them were down here in the loser zone.

She'd barely taken a sip when warm, warm fingers curled around her bicep. "Come on," Rafe said, his voice low. "Let's get out of here."

5

SHE DIDN'T SAY A WORD, simply let him pull her by the arm to one of the big French doors that led to a stone patio.

They were outside almost before she realized where he was taking her. He'd left the door ajar and they could hear the countdown begin.

Ten, Nine, Eight. He stared at her as though she were a rocket about to launch. Come to think of it, he wasn't far off. Still, it was the middle of winter and nearly midnight.

"Rafe, it's freezing out here."

He had his jacket off and around her before they got to the count of three. She felt his warmth, his scent, and stared up into his dark, dark eyes and stepped closer.

Two…one… All the noisemakers went off at once along with shouts of "Happy New Year!"

"Happy New Year, Arianne," Rafe said, his voice low and husky.

She tipped her face up, waiting for the New Year's kiss to end all New Year's kisses. Her eyes drifted shut, and she felt his fingers at the back of her head. He removed her mask…ooh, yes, transformation time.

Her foolishness in the bathroom came back to her and her lips curved as she felt the rush of cold air against her skin where the mask had been.

''You're releasing my female power, you know,'' she warned him.

''Damn, I hope so,'' he said, and then his mouth came down on hers.

How could the man's lips be so hot when it was so cold out here? She didn't know, but they were, pulling her in, as the winter night air pushed her closer to his heat. She wrapped her arms around his neck and his tuxedo jacket fell to the ground, but she didn't notice.

His arms were wrapped around her, his lips so hot and demanding against hers. She opened to him, needing more, and his tongue teased her, knowing what she needed, just about knocking her off last year's black Monticellos.

''What do you want, Arianne?'' he asked when he pulled away on a ragged breath.

His mouth was wet from kissing her, his eyes feverish.

''You, tonight,'' she said, throwing all caution to the cold wind that snapped around the patio.

Being spontaneous was like that. No tomorrow, no thought to consequences, no checks and balances, debits and credits. No bottom line.

''Are you sure?''

Her answer was to lick his throat.

He didn't ask a second time, but led her rapidly across the patio and through another French door.

This one led to the dining room where a cold buffet was already laid out. Soon, everyone would be eating a midnight supper, but for now it was deserted except for a couple of waiters standing ready to carve beef and ham. Platters of antipasto, salmon, pastas of all sorts, salads and breads covered banquet tables waiting for the post-midnight supper.

They sped through the room, with something other

than food on their minds, the waiters remaining as impassive as Buckingham Palace guards.

He led her, not out the main entrance, but through the kitchen, where the catering staff were busy at work.

Her heart was hammering. This was it. How long had she wanted Rafe? Her desire for him must have been flickering like a pilot light for it to burst into flaming life so suddenly.

Oh, she wanted him more than she'd ever wanted anything, or anyone.

They emerged into a hallway that was at once more modern and far less opulent than the parts of the house she'd seen before.

"The old servants' quarters," he explained, as they ran up a flight of stairs. "I had them made over into my quarters."

Contemporary, high-tech, sleek, but still luxurious, is what she thought when he pushed a security code, and they entered his private area.

She had only the vaguest impression of a comfortable living area, an entire wall of computer, TV and music stuff before he dragged her through another door and into his bedroom.

"When you say spontaneous, you mean spontaneous," she said, short of breath. She'd never seen him so lacking in manners or restraint and she really liked his lack of control now.

Her female power was so high and so potent she tingled with it. Obviously, he was under her spell. Probably, like most spells, this one would wear off along with the champagne or darkness.

Daylight would return, as would her senses. She'd spend the rest of her life living down her indiscretion.

When she tried to imagine how she'd feel, she decided she didn't care.

She'd have the memories. She'd know that once in her life she'd been as wild and spontaneous as she had it in her to be.

Rafe turned to her and stared at her as though he didn't quite know how to begin. He was always in control, so she found his momentary awkwardness rather touching.

His bedroom was surprisingly simple. Austere almost. There was the bed, a huge affair with a simple cotton duvet in a silvery gray color, a night table on which a half-read thriller novel sat, and a hardcover in Italian.

The bedside lamp was sleek and clearly designed for reading rather than ornamentation. Instead of a clothes closet, he had built-in cupboards and drawers, and through a half-open door she glimpsed a bathroom done in black-and-white.

He took one step closer to her and halted, yanking at his bow tie as though it were choking him. He had it open in no time, the ends dangling over his crisp white shirt like untied shoelaces.

Then awkwardness deserted him and he pulled her into his arms once more.

Oh, the heat that punched through her system was immediate and, if anything, stronger than out on the patio.

His hands slid over her back, warm and sure, while she pulled his head down to hers for another deep, wet kiss.

"I knew when we danced together it was going to be like this," she said when they stopped to breathe.

"How is it going to be?" he asked, his voice husky.

She smiled. "Amazing."

"I always knew it would be amazing with you," he said, so softly he could have been speaking to himself.

He had? He'd thought about this before? Well, she supposed she had felt…something, but she'd always assumed it was just the result of his charm and that it happened to all the women he met.

Pushing the thought of all the women he…met out of her mind with great firmness, she went back to kissing him.

There were shirt studs to deal with, a cummerbund to remove. She couldn't waste her energy on anything but what was happening right now in this room.

She sighed as she went to work, enjoying the act of undressing him, of taking him from the epitome of civilized in his tuxedo, to naked and animal.

Beneath the crisp whiteness of the shirt, his chest hair emerged as soft as a wolf's pelt.

Off came his shirt, and she touched him everywhere, glorying in muscles that had both climbed mountains and dived beneath the ocean. She buried her face against his chest and caressed him with the tip of her tongue.

"Mmm," she said. "You smell Italian."

He chuckled, the muscles quivering beneath her lips. "What does Italian smell like?"

She breathed in again, closing her eyes. "Like olive oil, and herbs drying in the sun. Basil and rosemary."

"You make me sound like a pizza."

She licked again, finding a flat brown nipple and teasing it. "I love pizza."

He ran his hands through her hair, down her back, until his fingers were working the closure at the back of her dress. "And you smell like something cool and fresh. A layer of fresh snow on a mountaintop."

She frowned slightly. "Snow is awfully cold."

"Until it melts." And with a flick of his wrist, he released her dress and it slipped down her front. Without any nice shapely hips to stop it, the dress picked up speed and slid to the floor like a toboggan down that mountain slope he'd likened her to.

He didn't seem to mind her lack of curves, though. The sound he made as he gazed at her body, naked but for a pair of black silk panties, made any hesitation she felt disappear. It was as if the breath had been knocked out of him.

Feeling desire bubble beneath the surface of her skin, she moaned softly when he palmed her breasts. Once more she was assailed by heat. His hands were leathery from gripping climbing ropes, ski poles, horse reins and bike handlebars. They'd fought rapids and mountain heights and they'd picked up his mother's shoes and turned a business into an empire.

He slid those amazing hands down her torso, hooked his thumbs in the waistband of her panties and pulled them off.

She shivered, but not from cold. He was so warm, she didn't think she'd ever feel cold when they were together. She trembled from the knowledge that this was different.

If anyone ever asked her again about wild, spontaneous sex she knew she wouldn't have to reach into her fantasy bank for a story.

Not that she planned to share this one. It was going to be hers alone.

He set her on the bed and knelt, kissing her ankle before undoing her shoe. "Your feet were made for our shoes," he said.

She smiled at his foolishness and offered him the other, which he removed with just as much ceremony.

She moved up the bed until she could flip the duvet back and slip onto rich linen sheets. She didn't jump right in and cover herself as she might on another occasion.

Since this was only going to last a short time, she figured she ought to enjoy the moment to its fullest.

"You're wearing entirely too many clothes," she informed him.

One side of his mouth kicked up as he stared down at her stretched out for him like a smorgasbord as though he couldn't believe her lack of shyness.

She couldn't believe it, either, but in that moment, she felt feminine modesty was overrated.

There was no need for a second hint. His slacks, briefs, socks and shoes all came off in under five seconds. Then he rose and took a step toward the bed.

"Wait," she commanded. "I haven't finished looking."

She wanted to study him the way an art student might study a famous sculpture. A famous sculpture of a tongue-drippingly gorgeous naked man.

Even though her fingers itched to touch him and discover whether his muscles felt as elastic as they looked, his skin as smooth as it appeared, his erection as thick, for a moment she just wanted to look. She'd always suspected he'd look fantastic naked, and he did. He looked better than fantastic.

His shoulders were broad, his arms defined, his belly taut, his chest hair curled provocatively around terracotta-colored nipples, and lower down the hair was a shade darker, making his erection appear pale as marble.

Not white marble, though, more like gold-colored Siena marble. It looked as hard as marble, too. All her womanly parts softened and opened, already anticipating that hardness within her. Oh, how she wanted it.

She'd managed to drag her gaze down to his thighs, which were very nice as thighs went but nowhere near as exciting as his groin area, when he made a tiny sound.

Glancing at his face she discovered heightened color across his cheekbones. "Are you finished? I feel like a damned science experiment."

He was blushing.

She was so surprised, she laughed and held out her hand. Of course, his momentary discomfort hadn't stopped him from staring at her as avidly as she'd stared at him.

Her skin felt warmed by his gaze. Her blood heated by it.

He joined her on the bed, and she was glad she'd looked when she had the chance, for he immediately pulled her tight against him, and she might as well have been blind for all she could see.

She shut her eyes anyway, so it didn't matter. The sense that dominated now was touch.

Everywhere their bodies brushed, she felt heat penetrating, building.

He surrounded her in warmth, and she felt as though she were melting.

"I want to touch you all over," he murmured, as his lips cruised her throat and headed for her breasts. "I want to taste you everywhere," he added, and then took a nipple into his mouth, flicking it with his tongue before pulling with gentle suction.

She gasped as the same suction echoed at the very core of her. Desire flowed strong and hot, moving south as his tongue trailed a path over her belly and down.

She was moaning helplessly when he parted her thighs and slipped between.

When he touched her with his tongue, a long, slow lick, she shuddered. He didn't tease her, for which she was grateful, but he didn't rush her along, either, simply took the time to taste and explore, always returning to her burning clit with those long, slow, ice-cream-cone licks that built her up and up.

When she'd tossed her head about on the pillow so much that her hair was snapping with static electricity, he cupped her hips in his big, hot hands and tongued her to a deliberate, pulsing rhythm.

The tension within her was building, roaring in her ears when he increased the pressure and speed of his movements. She felt such a power surge she damn near shorted out.

That banshee wail echoing off the walls couldn't be coming from cool and controlled Arianne Sorenson, could it?

She raised up onto her elbows to see if there was somebody else in the room screaming her head off, but her gaze encountered only Rafe grinning up at her, his head so dark against her white limbs.

He kissed his way up her body while she tried to catch her breath and slow her slamming heart. She wondered how much more of this she could survive.

While she contemplated the fact that his male power was running pretty potent tonight, as well, he leaned over her and grabbed a condom from his bedside table.

"Wait," she said. "I want to do that."

What she really wanted was to touch him, unencumbered by latex.

He handed her the condom and she pushed him onto his back then encircled him with one hand. As she'd suspected, he was hard as marble, but much, much warmer.

His skin was silk-soft over his stiff erection, and she took a moment to enjoy all the textures. The smoothest skin was at the tip, which she circled with her index finger. She traced her way down his just-as-smooth shaft until she reached coarse springy hair. The sac was as leathery and alive as the skin wrinkled and shifted under her hands.

If she'd almost screamed herself into passing out, Rafe sounded as though he might pant himself into unconsciousness.

She smiled a little as she bent down and took him into her mouth. Mmm. He tasted good. Once more she thought of warmed olive oil and fresh herbs baking in the sun. No, not pizza, she thought fuzzily, but focaccia.

Thinking about food and flavors got her a little busier with her tongue than she'd intended.

From what seemed a long way off she heard a groan and a curse in Italian. Suddenly, Rafe flipped her onto her back so fast she almost swallowed her tongue.

"You took too long," he complained, grabbing the condom and sheathing himself.

"I almost made you lose control," she corrected, noting the sweat beading his forehead and the ragged breathing of an extreme athlete who's reached his extreme.

"Yeah."

He kissed her and along with the excitement that still ran so high in her body, she felt a rush of tenderness that made her wrap her arms around him and cling. She'd come so far, she couldn't back out now, but it occurred to her that once Rafe entered her body, nothing was going to be the same.

6

"OPEN FOR ME," he said softly.

"Yes," she whispered, feeling her body do just that without any conscious effort. As greedily as her mouth had opened on his tongue, so now did her body open for him.

She slipped her legs wide apart, and he moved between them until she felt the blunt probing of his cock, amazingly hot.

"Yes," she said again as their gazes locked.

He entered her slowly, and as she accepted him inside of her all the pieces of her life suddenly felt as if they clicked into place. All those jigsaw-puzzle-piece moments of decision. Moving to New York, volunteering for the charity auction, ending her engagement to Charlie, going to work for Rafe, the way they'd teased, flirted, danced.

So many images suddenly fit together into a single one that made sense. The pair of them connected in this intimate, magical way.

He began to move and she moved with him, as perfectly, harmoniously in time with each other as they had been on the dance floor.

He held her tight, and pushed up inside her, seeming to drive deeper with each thrust.

That power—her magical female power—was building again, flowing through her body.

Power was building inside Rafe, too. Faster and stronger. So fast she needed to cling to him, wrap her arms and legs hard around him to stop from flying into a million pieces.

But, of course, there was no way to stop it and suddenly she was doing just that. Flying into a million separate, sparkling pieces. Her entire being burst into glitter—like one of the fireworks she could hear exploding outside.

As her climax rocked her, she felt Rafe's own fireworks as he shuddered and pulsed deep inside her body.

Tears came from nowhere to sting at the corners of her eyes. She was moved to her very depths by what had just happened, floating on a wave of contentment.

I love you.

Her eyes flew open and her body clenched with embarrassment. Had she said those words aloud? Oh, lord. What was she thinking? A woman like her didn't blurt out declarations of love to a man like Rafe just because they'd had sex together. How naive, how provincial how...true.

He was muttering in Italian. *"Come cazzo mi fai impazzire,"* and something else she couldn't understand. It sounded like *piano.* He whispered the words, kissing her eyes, her cheeks and finally her mouth. She didn't know what all of it meant, but *cazzo* was one of those words he used when he was angry about something. A curse.

In spite of the soft kisses, she could imagine what the words were in translation.

She turned her face away from his too-warm and inviting lips. She wanted to roll into a ball and sob.

The truth was devastating. She, Arianne Sorenson,

tried one time, once in twenty-seven years to be wild and spontaneous and it ended in disaster.

She, who spent her life preaching prudence, budgeting, sensible investments for the long term, checks and balances, had taken a flyer. Bet her life savings on a whim.

She'd fallen in love with a womanizing playboy.

Where she'd reveled in her nakedness before, now she felt miserably shy and awkward. She wanted to turn back the clock, to go back to the moment she'd had a premonition and tried to turn back from the party.

Isabel and Nat had talked her into going ahead and they'd never given her worse advice.

"Arianne?" Rafe smoothed his hand over her hair, the pale gold strands silky-smooth to the touch. "What is it?"

She'd turned from a wild, soft, giving woman to a plank in the space of five seconds.

"Could you maybe move off me? I think I'm getting claustrophobia," she said in a small voice, addressing his sock drawer rather than him.

He rolled to the side, but didn't get out of bed. Instead he took her chin and pulled until she was looking at him. "Better?"

"Yes, thanks." She didn't look better, she looked as though something really, really bad had just happened to her. Now, Rafe was probably as insensitive as the next red-blooded male, at least if women's magazine headlines were to be believed, but he didn't think their lovemaking could be causing the tragic expression on her face.

Hell, they should be out there whooping and hollering with the rest of the New Year's revelers. They'd touched the bloody stars, he and Arianne. What wasn't terrific about that?

"Tell me. What is it?"

"What was the last thing you heard me say?" she asked him quietly.

Okay, something was going on here. He had no idea what she wanted him to say, but the best he could manage was giving her the courtesy of being honest. "Let's see." He traced the undersides of her pert breasts with a finger, drawing a shallow *W*. "I think it was yes."

"Yes? That's the last thing I said? You're sure?"

"Well, if you want the complete replay, it was *Yes, oh, Rafe, yes, Rafe, yes…*"

He could hear her now, her cries looping through his head like the favorite line of a favorite song. It wasn't just the words, but the tone of them. Chanted to the same rhythm as her thrusting hips. She had sounded amazed, thrilled…awed. He knew, because he'd felt the same emotions.

His answer seemed to satisfy her, for she lost the rigid set to her jaw, but he didn't need to be a sensitive new-age guy to realize there wasn't going to be another round of gravity-defying lovemaking anytime soon. It was as though she'd withdrawn.

She'd shut her glorious passion away in some icebox of her own making, and he didn't have a clue what that was about. Puzzled, annoyed, and even a bit hurt, he wondered what more a woman could want from him than a declaration of love.

Or was that the problem?

"Do you remember my last words?" he asked.

She glanced at him. "They were in Italian."

"Really?" He started to laugh. His mother would be delighted. A man who made love to the woman of his heart in Italian would father a lot of kids. "Do you want a translation?" He felt a little weird asking her. A couple of minutes ago when things were warm and they'd been as closely connected as two people could be, he'd felt natural expressing his love. But now that she'd turned cold, it seemed an awful risk. Still, if she wanted to know, he'd tell her.

Instead, she sent him an icy, close-lipped smile. "No thanks. I've heard those words before. You always curse in Italian."

He sat up in bed so fast his head spun. She thought he'd been cursing? They'd touched some new universe together; how could she believe he'd...

There was no point wondering. She was already out of bed, dressing with the same frantic haste he'd used in undressing her.

He watched her from the bed. With his hands stacked beneath his head, his position may have looked casual, but really it was to stop them from breaking something.

"Stay," he said.

She glanced at him, pale and startled, as though he were speaking a foreign language. Again.

"Stay," he repeated. "With me. Tonight."

"But you're the host."

"My mother will do a brilliant job without me."

"But, but...if I stay the night, your mother will know...Isabel and Natalie will know." She was growing paler and paler. In a minute or so she was just going to disappear. "Everyone will know."

He was getting a bad feeling in his gut. "Everyone will know what?"

"That I...that we..."

"Made love? Had sex? Screwed? F—"

"Stop it! I know what we did. I just don't want everyone in the five boroughs to know." She shoved her feet into her shoes blindly and stumbled toward the door.

He rolled out of bed and stalked her so fast she

jumped. "Don't forget all the old boys at the Italian-American club, and everybody I'll e-mail about my latest conquest."

She flapped about like a flustered white dove. "Stop it! I don't mean that, I'm just not ready, I don't want… I can't…"

Even through his sudden fury he could see she was in serious emotional distress. Maybe those women's magazines were right after all. Men and women were never going to get each other. The sex he and Arianne had had tonight made him want to weep with joy and start planning the wedding. It seemed to be sending Arianne straight to a shrink's couch.

He grabbed her shoulders as gently as he could considering he wanted to shake some sense into her. Once he had her immobile and glaring at him, he said, "If you go downstairs like that you're going to fall and break your neck. Your shoes aren't done up. And if you survive that, anyone will take one look at you and see what you've been doing.

"Personally, I'm proud of what happened. Since you don't feel that way, give me five minutes to get dressed and out of here and you can take your time. The bathroom's through there. You can fix your hair and stuff. There are fresh towels in there." He gestured to a bank of cupboards.

She nodded. "Thanks."

He was as good as his word. In less than five minutes he was back in his tux and heading out the door.

Since he didn't know what to say, he decided not to say anything.

At the door she stopped him.

"I'm not ashamed of what happened," she said softly. "I'm confused."

"You're confusing the hell out of me, too."

7

FOR THE SECOND TIME that evening, Arianne found herself staring at herself in one of the Monticello house mirrors. Sometime between the first mirror and the second, all her female power seemed to have drained away. Fizzled. Evaporated.

She sighed. She had raccoon eyes and smudged lipstick to deal with as well as rat's-nest hair.

Thank goodness Rafe had stopped her from rejoining the party in her current state. She shuddered and walked to the cupboard where he'd told her the towels were kept.

She opened the burled maple door and found not towels, but ties, socks, underwear, and shirts, all in fitted drawers and shelves of the same wood.

She paused for a moment to enjoy the faint scent of Rafe that clung to his things.

Arianne was so embarrassed she'd been such an idiot, that she'd been stupid enough to fall in love with a man she could never have. Sniffing his clean laundry seemed pretty minor by comparison.

Either Rafe or some efficient member of the house staff was very neat. Everything was in perfect order. Ties were arranged by color, shirts hung at attention, whites first, then the colors. She was about to close the door and try the next one for towels when a scrap of pale blue caught her eye from the drawer beneath the one that contained his socks.

She pulled it open, and her eyes opened wide.

No wonder it had seemed as though the blue silk didn't fit with the rest of the items in this closet. It was a woman's camisole.

And it was perfect. Clearly it had never been worn, for the tag was still attached. She peeked and frowned. Three thousand dollars? Maybe the silkworms had been singing the "Hallelujah Chorus" when they spun this silk, because it was so rich, so soft and touchable that she couldn't resist playing the fabric between her thumb and finger.

An ice-blue camisole, three thousand dollars. He didn't buy those in bulk at Costco. She remembered perfectly well teasing him about the item, and about the lady friend for whom he'd purchased it. He'd certainly given Arianne the impression it had been gratefully received and well worn.

She hadn't thought she could feel any more confused, but now she did. Confused and wretched. What a way to start a whole new year.

Once she was tidied up and had repaired everything but her shredded heart, she crept back downstairs and slipped into the still-partying throng.

But, if she'd ever been in a party mood, she no longer was.

Across the room she caught a glimpse of Natalie in the arms of a tough, quiet-looking man. They appeared to be more than new friends. Natalie couldn't seem to keep her eyes—or her hands—off him. Interesting.

Arianne made her way over, and tapped Nat on the shoulder. "Listen, I've got a headache. I think I'll grab a cab home now."

"Everything okay?"

She forced a smile. "Yes. Of course. I'll tell you everything tomorrow at Isabel's." They'd already arranged to have New Year's Day brunch at Isabel's SoHo loft. As much as she wanted to spill her problems right now, she knew she'd have to wait. Natalie clearly had something on the go with the tough-guy hunk she so obviously wasn't introducing to Arianne.

"Tell Isabel goodbye for me when she surfaces. And Happy New Year."

They hugged each other, and then she slipped out.

A polite person would thank Rafe and his mother for their hospitality. To hell with it. A polite person could send a card. Much more her style. Polite and impersonal.

She began composing it in her head.

Dear Rafe,
    Thank you for a lovely evening. The sex was particularly exciting.

Cordially yours, Arianne.

There was nothing spontaneous about a woman who used words like *cordially,* which had such a distant, old-fashioned ring to it, and who wrote formal thank-you notes.

And Arianne had just decided she was never, ever doing spontaneous again.

Plans, controls, checks and balances. Order. That was for her. None of this willy-nilly tossing caution to the wind and her heart to a man who collected them like bottle caps.

When she got to the coat check, she gave her name and asked them to call her a cab. She accepted her coat, and the attendant also handed her the trademark gold Monticello shoe box that she knew contained this year's pair of black shoes—the closest thing to sensible you could get in the Monticello line.

She squelched an impulse to turn down the gift. That would only arouse comment she was anxious to avoid, so she tried to smile and appear delighted.

By the time she arrived home, her headache was no longer feigned. She gulped a couple of painkillers, tried to ignore the sounds of merriment that continued out on the streets and undressed and slipped into pajamas.

She crawled into bed, but her cold single-girl sheets only reminded her of the feel of Rafe's sheets against her skin, his hot body moving against hers. How warm she'd been when Rafe had shared the bed.

She slapped her hands over her face and did a groan, howl, sob combo.

After a long time spent listening to everyone in Manhattan but her having the time of their lives, she sat up and flipped on the light.

A glow of gold from the corner of her room caught her attention and she padded barefoot to open her box of shoes. Might as well take a peek.

She slipped the lid off—even the box was so expensive she handled it with care—expecting to see shoes the color of her mood. Solid, unrelieved black.

She gasped and blinked. Nestled inside a layer of tissue was a pair of strappy red shoes with crystal-studded ankle bands.

Wild, sassy, party-girl shoes.

The kind of shoes a spontaneous, exciting, confident woman would wear. The kind of shoes Arianne would wear if she were to sneak off with Rafe Monticello in the middle of a party after telling him she wanted to make love with him.

A tiny smile lit her face. The kind of woman she'd

been for a couple of hours tonight. Before she'd so stupidly tumbled into love.

She eased one shoe, then the other out of the box. They were her size, but still she was convinced that there'd been a mistake, or that they'd run out of black shoes and had to substitute red.

She pulled out the enclosed card, expecting the pre-printed Happy New Year's card from the whole Monticello family, but instead there was a handwritten card on Rafe's own stationery—the stuff he brought in at an exorbitant price from Europe.

Darling Arianne,
 Take a chance and follow your heart. Have dinner with me. I'll pick you up at eight o'clock.
 Love, Rafe.

She flapped the stiff handmade paper under her chin trying to dispel the rush of heat that suffused her.

She read the note again. While she'd been inventing thank-you-for-the-sex notes in her head and signing them "cordially, Arianne," he'd been penning a real in-his-own-writing-on-his-special-paper note and he'd signed it *Love, Rafe.*

And he wanted to see her again tomorrow.

She slipped the shoes on and tightened the straps. Then she tottered to her full-length mirror and hoisted up her pajama pant legs and turned this way and that, inspecting the shoes from every angle.

No matter how she looked at them, they were still red high heels that sent out all sorts of messages about her.

A woman wearing shoes like this wasn't cautious. A woman in shoes like these wasn't sensible. A woman in shoes like this was…insane.

Oh, God. What had she done? What was she going to do?

Could she plunge into an affair with the most exciting man she'd ever known? A man who would show her a wonderful time, treat her with charm and generosity and then tire of her? Could she do that with a man she loved?

Fortunately, she'd clung to just enough sanity to reach for the one lifeline she knew she could count on.

Still wearing the shoes, she danced across the room to her phone and left the same message on two machines.

"It's me, Arianne. Huge emergency. We have to move brunch up to eleven."

They had to meet earlier because depending on Natalie and Isabel's verdict on the shoes and the dinner invitation, Arianne had to go shopping.

She gulped as she stared down at the shoes, winking at her like a promise.

She wasn't going to go picking through last season's leftovers, either. She raised her head and pulled back her shoulders. She was heading for the full-price racks of the newest trends.

8

THE SKIRT OF the ridiculous red dress Iz had lent her was flirting with Arianne's thighs.

It teased, caressed, tickled and generally reminded her that there were a couple of miles of leg between the soft chiffon-silk dress and her new Monticellos. And, in case anyone missed that fact, the dress, like the shoes, was in head-turning red.

It was the silliest, most impractical outfit Arianne had ever owned. It matched the silliest, most impractical pair of shoes she'd ever owned, and she loved them both.

She'd been mildly horrified when Nat and Isabel had bullied and manhandled her into trying on clothes—making her feel like a well-played-with fashion doll—until they were satisfied with the results.

Once she'd explained about last night and the camisole, Isabel—after suggesting Rafe might be a cross-dresser—had jumped in with enthusiasm. And, once she got into the spirit of things, Arianne had to admit the three of them had had fun playing dress-up.

She only wished the others were here now to give her a few more laughs and build up her confidence.

She'd left her hair down so it swung softly against her jawline. Not content with the dress, she'd even given herself a manicure and pedicure so her nails gleamed bold red.

Now she waited, for once cursing her habit of being so punctual. It was only five to eight.

She picked up a magazine and had to resist gnawing off the crimson nail polish. She tugged the dress down a little, wishing her stomach wasn't a knot of nerves. Wishing she'd had more sleep last night. Wishing she knew what the hell she was going to say when Rafe arrived.

When her intercom buzzed she was no closer to knowing what she wanted to say to him than she had been before.

Follow your heart, his note had suggested. Follow it where? To Paris for the weekend? To the chichi clubs he frequented? The parties? The restaurants? To the final Tiffany-boxed goodbye?

She opened the door, and he stood before her, dark and sexy and altogether wonderful.

He blinked.

Oh, God. She never should have listened to Natalie. It was too much red. "I know," she said, pulling the hem down to hide a bit more leg. "I look like a fire engine."

"You look," he said, "incredible. I fantasized about you in those shoes."

"You did?" She licked her lips, knowing in that moment she'd follow him to the broken heart stage because she couldn't help herself. "What were we doing in your fantasy?"

He stepped forward until their bodies touched. "I'll show you."

The door banged shut behind him and she didn't even notice. She was in his arms and they were kissing as though they'd been separated for months. She couldn't get close enough, touch enough, hug enough of him to her.

His hands were everywhere, skimming the red silk,

trailing warm fingers over every bit of her skin he could reach, tracing the hem of her skirt until she giggled. And kissing her. Always kissing her.

"Dinner later?" he managed to say, when she'd dragged his jacket off and tossed it on her couch. Her dress was askew and only one barely-there spaghetti strap kept it from falling to the floor.

"Dinner, later," she agreed.

While she worked at his shirt buttons, he pulled out a cell phone and punched a key. "Raoul, move the dinner reservation to ten-thirty, will you? Come back for us at ten."

He pocketed the phone and then reached for the spaghetti strap.

How nice to have a limo driver at your beck and call, she thought. Then her dress floated to the ground like a stripper's scarf, and she forgot to think at all.

"Red panties, too. Nice."

"I like my outfits to match," she explained in a voice that trembled slightly with need and nerves.

She'd never made love with a man she loved this deeply before. She wasn't sure what it would do to her.

"These come off," he said, hooking his thumbs in her panties. "But these," he indicated the absurd shoes, "stay on."

They never made it to the bedroom.

Rafe turned her, and she took one step before lust slammed into him. There was no way he could walk as far as the bedroom with that naked ass, pushed higher than normal by the red heels, swaying in front of him without doing himself permanent injury.

One step, two, three... He let her go, imprinting the sight on his brain, then came up behind her and wrapped an arm around her waist, pulling her back against his body. Her round butt pushed against his erection and he felt sweat break out on his forehead.

"Stay." He managed to croak the word. "Here."

He was out of his clothes in record time, then holding her again to feel her lush, bare ass against him. He reached round and cupped her breasts, playing with them.

She pushed against him and rubbed her butt cheeks back and forth across his cock. More sweat broke out and he stifled a moan.

He was so desperate for her he was losing control.

Slipping one hand down her belly to cup her heat, he found she was already slick, the folds of her sex swollen.

Excitement surged through him. She was as close as he was. Even as his fingers started to play with her, she panted and her butt started to wiggle against him.

Because he'd had such high hopes for tonight, there was a condom in his wallet. In seconds he had it on.

Then he bent her over the side of the couch and thrust, deep and hard into that incredible, wet woman's place he'd been obsessing about revisiting.

She cried out with surprise, and he held very still for a moment, enjoying the way she clung to him. Tight and hot inside, much hotter than her cool exterior would have led him to believe.

Once more he reached round and slipped his hand between the couch arm and her body, rubbing that perfect spot as he started to thrust. Almost all the way out and then in again. With each movement his hips slapped her soft round cheeks. The muscles of her back danced and flexed as she pushed mindlessly with her arms, arching her back each time he entered her.

He held himself tightly in check until he heard those magic words. "Oh, yes. Rafe. Yes. Yes, Rafe, yes…"

Then he let himself go, exploding deep inside her body

until he saw stars, telling her his love in words as well as with his body. *"Dio, come cazzo ti amo."*

With the last of his strength, he dragged both of them onto the couch where they flopped, him on the bottom, her sprawled on top of him.

As they floated back to earth he became aware that rivulets of water were running down his chest.

Not even a jog up Everest could produce that much sweat, and he didn't think she'd scratched an artery and he was bleeding, so he had to go with the most unpleasant possibility.

"Are you crying?"

She sniffled in reply, too broken up to speak.

"Happy tears?" he asked hopefully.

The blond head shook. A definite no.

He cursed softly and fluently in Italian. "You have the damnedest responses to great sex. I can't imagine what you do if it's bad."

"It's not that," she sobbed. "It's not the sex."

He sure hoped not. Although he'd been pretty raunchy, borderline rough, it felt as if she'd been with him all the way. Right down to the stunning home stretch. Still, he had to consider the possibility.

"Did I hurt you?"

Again she shook her head. "The sex was fantastic," she sobbed.

Okay. Whatever was going on here wasn't physical. It was emotional.

He didn't mind emotion. Hell, he was Italian. He had a few of his own, but she had to tell him what he was dealing with. Was that too much to ask?

Not happy. "Are you sad?"

Louder sobbing. Great, fantastic. The woman turned

earth-shattering sex into a tragedy. Wasn't anything ever simple with Arianne?

"Talk to me, why are you sad?"

She buried her face in his neck and mumbled, "Because I'm so stupid. I can't be one of your women. I can't." The way she wailed the last word it seemed to echo.

"What do you mean one of my women?" He'd barely got his breath back, and she was throwing out emotional zingers.

"The ice-blue camisole in your wardrobe. Who's that for?"

He was distracted by the pale shoulder hunched so protectively against him. He thought he'd never seen anything so sad as that one shoulder.

"Ice-blue camisole?" She was sobbing over underwear?

"In your wardrobe." She sniffled. "Could you pass me a tissue please?" He plucked a couple from the box on her side table and gave them to her. She muttered her thanks without turning her head.

"What camisole?"

"I didn't snoop, but I opened the wrong door looking for towels and there were your socks and underwear and this camisole. Three thousand dollars. You told me you bought it for Anita, way back in September."

He remembered now, and his own foolishness amazed him.

"I never told you I bought it for Anita. I may have let you assume that, but it wasn't true."

He didn't often feel embarrassed, but he did now. Why hadn't he given the stupid thing to one of his sisters?

"Who did you buy it for?"

He'd never felt a bigger fool in his life. "You," he admitted grumpily. "I bought it for you."

She sniffed again, louder. "But you didn't know I'd…you didn't know we'd…"

He couldn't just sit here like a fool while the woman he loved turned a truly cold shoulder on him. He had to tell her the truth.

"I was in L.A. and saw it. I thought it would look great on you…so I bought it. I don't know, I guess I thought that even if you were always bugging me about my dates, you were thinking of me in that way and maybe one day you'd think of us together in that way." He almost winced with humiliation. What an ass he'd been.

Well, he'd gone this far. The evening was, to date, mostly a replay of the night before. Great sex followed by profound misery. Might as well get it all out in the open.

He rolled off the couch, leaned down to pick up his jacket off the floor and pulled out the box. He laid it on a feminine floral pillow beside her head, which was currently turned into the back of the couch. "I brought you something."

Once more her sobs increased. If she cried any harder she was going to burst something. "Is it a T-T-Tiffany's box?"

Dread clenched his chest. She wanted Tiffany's? Maybe he'd been wrong about Arianne. Maybe…

"Could you just open it? Please?"

She flapped her hand behind her and said, "Tissue."

He obliged. She wiped her eyes and sat up, so naked and so beautiful, her face pale but calm. "I'd like to see the box."

He passed it to her. The velvet was worn and had once

been royal blue, he suspected, but was now the color of faded denim.

She blinked and frowned when she saw it, running a finger over a bald patch on the velvet. "This isn't from Tiffany's," she said in amazement.

"No." His throat was clogged with all the things he wanted to say and didn't know how, with all the things he was beginning to fear.

She flipped it open and didn't say a single word.

He started to babble. "We can get something from Tiffany's or anywhere else you like. But that was my grandmother's ring. She gave it to me for my wife. It would mean a lot to me if you'd wear—"

"Your wife?" she asked as though it were a word with which she was unfamiliar.

Oh, he was botching this, and badly. "I'm doing a piss-poor job of it, but I am asking you to marry me."

The single ruby, rich and red, glowed in the simple gold setting. Most women wore diamonds on their engagement fingers. He knew that. He didn't care. He'd fill her fingers with diamonds, he just wanted Arianne.

"You don't have to wear it if you don't like it."

"I love it." She sniffed again and another tear tracked down her face.

"Then why are you crying now?"

"These," she said, pointing, "are happy tears."

The pressure on his chest eased. "Happy tears are good, right?"

She nodded, spilling a whole bucketful of happy down her face.

"So you'll marry me?"

She nodded, too choked to speak, and he felt happiness sting his own eyes.

He dropped his gaze to the ring and withdrew it from

the box. "My grandparents were married for sixty-three years," he told her as he slipped the ring onto her left hand.

"That sounds like a good number," she said, sinking into his arms for a kiss. "What about children?"

His heart swelled as he pictured Arianne pregnant with their child.

"I'm Italian, male and Catholic. What do you think?"

She smiled a prim smile that went wicked at the corners. "I think we'd better get married very soon."

"Now you're talking."

"Rafe?"

"Mmm?"

"You've never told me you loved me."

He turned to stare at her. "I've told you twice and both times you started sobbing. You scared me off."

"You did not. You've never said the words to me."

"Ti amo," he said, nice and loud, putting his all into it.

Her blue eyes blinked wide. "You never said that before."

He tried to remember what he'd shouted out in passion. He was sure he'd said he loved her. He'd certainly been thinking it. "What did I say?"

She blushed a little and dropped her gaze. "Something with *cazzo* in it. I know because it's what you say when you're cursing."

"Curses?" He started to laugh. "I was telling you I love you in a very earthy way. I do. I love your mind, who you are, and I definitely love your body."

"Oh. Thank you."

"You've never said the words, either. In any language."

"I said them in my head, the first time we made love. That's when I realized I was in love with you."

"Is that why you started crying?"

She nodded.

"I still want to hear them."

"*Jag älskar dej.* I love you, Rafe."

EPILOGUE

Epilogue

One year later

THE ANNUAL MONTICELLO Ball was still in full swing long after the hour of celebration had passed. In a quiet corner of the deserted bar far from the remaining party-goers, Arianne, Isabel and Natalie gathered for a New Year's toast.

"We weren't sure you'd be here," Arianne said. Taking Natalie's hand, she admired the princess-cut diamond ring Natalie sported. "It's supposed to be your wedding night."

Natalie laughed. "And miss out on a new pair of Monticellos?" She lovingly smoothed her hand over the signature gold box resting on the bar. "Are you nuts?"

"Nuts is a woman who'd leave a yummy guy like Joe alone on his honeymoon," Isabel joked. She gave Natalie a quick hug. "Um, so...how does marriage feel?" The question betrayed enough of a cautious, yet genuine, curiosity that Natalie and Arianne exchanged a knowing glance. Although Tom had practically moved into Isabel's loft, she never would admit that she'd fallen head over heels in love with him.

"The first twelve hours have been pretty spectacular," Natalie said. "Ask me again in another thirty years."

Natalie, always the romantic, had practically insisted on a New Year's Eve wedding when Joe proposed to her

Christmas morning. The poor man. He'd probably been thinking a year from now, not a week later before a justice of the peace. Natalie hadn't been about to give him a chance to disappear on her again, even if they had been living together since Valentine's Day.

Isabel focused on Arianne next. "We have a surprise for you, and don't think of arguing with us."

Arianne's expression changed to apprehension when Isabel handed her a large white envelope. When Isabel and Natalie put their devious minds together, just about anything was possible.

"Okay. It's a totally self-serving gift, but neither one of us can survive another one of your bargain-hunting trips," Natalie said.

Arianne opened the sealed envelope and withdrew a sketch of a wedding gown. The design was elegant, simple and feminine, with a swatch of cream silk attached to one corner with a pin. Arianne recognized Isabel's handiwork.

"Dupioni silk, sent straight from Italy," Isabel said with pride. "Hand-dyed. See the subtle embroidery and beadwork on the bodice? I designed the pattern."

Natalie jumped in. "It's just a sketch, so if you don't like it, you can change it however you want. But please, no more trips to those awful Jersey outlet warehouses."

Arianne peered closer. "Vera Wang!" she exclaimed in horror. Her mental calculator short-circuited.

Isabel nodded, beaming with the pleasure of getting to work alongside the famed designer.

Natalie's excitement bubbled over into her voice. "She owes Lucia a favor."

"Rafe's mother knows about this?" Arianne asked.

The two women laughed.

"She's designed the shoes to go with this gown," Isabel replied.

"Oh, it's gorgeous!" Arianne threw her arms around both women and gave them loud smackers on the cheek. "Thank you, but why are you doing this?"

"Hah! We figure if that red dress hooked Rafe," Isabel teased, "then this wedding gown should keep him."

"All right, now I'm an old married woman," Natalie said cheerfully, "and Arianne and Rafe's wedding is in six months…" She eyed Isabel. "Come on, Iz. When are you going to make Tom an honest man?"

Isabel shrugged in that careless way of hers and smiled a secret sort of smile that spiked Arianne's and Natalie's curiosity. They gasped when Isabel lifted the crystal champagne flute to her lips, turning so the twinkling lights overhead caught the reflection of the sapphire-and-diamond heirloom ring on her left hand.

A delighted Natalie leaned in for a closer look. "It's stunning!"

"When did this happen?" Arianne asked, her happiness for Isabel evident in her wide, beaming smile.

"When do you think?" Isabel gave them a naughty wink. "At the stroke of midnight."

HARLEQUIN®
Temptation

What happens when a girl finds herself in the *wrong* bed...with the *right* guy?

Find out in:

#866 NAUGHTY BY NATURE by Jule McBride
February 2002

#870 SOMETHING WILD by Toni Blake
March 2002

#874 CARRIED AWAY by Donna Kauffman
April 2002

#878 HER PERFECT STRANGER by Jill Shalvis
May 2002

#882 BARELY MISTAKEN by Jennifer LaBrecque
June 2002

#886 TWO TO TANGLE by Leslie Kelly
July 2002

Midnight mix-ups have never been so much fun!

HARLEQUIN®
Makes any time special ®

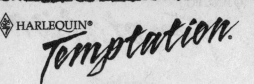
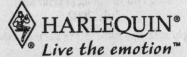

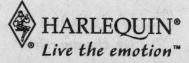

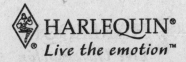